HEMLOCKED AND LOADED

SPELLBOUND PARANORMAL COZY MYSTERY,
BOOK 9

ANNABEL CHASE

RED PALM PRESS LLC

Hemlocked and Loaded

A Spellbound Paranormal Cozy Mystery, Book 9

By Annabel Chase

Sign up for my newsletter at http://eepurl.com/ctYNzf and or like me on Facebook **so you can find out about new releases.**

Copyright © 2017 Red Palm Press LLC

Cover Design by Alchemy

❀ Created with Vellum

CHAPTER 1

"So SPARKLY," Begonia said. Her pert face was mere inches from my ring finger.

"It's the way the light's hitting it," I said. The classroom of the ASS Academy was bathed in sunlight this morning.

"It could also be the fact that it's huge and perfectly formed," Begonia teased. "Did Daniel buy this from Deacon?" Deacon was a dwarf that owned Deacon's Stones, the most popular jewelry store in Spellbound.

"Yes, but we chose it together," I said. "We want this marriage to be a true partnership, so we're trying to make as many joint decisions as possible."

Millie eyed me suspiciously. "And does that include decisions about the wedding?"

"Absolutely," I said. "This is *not* going to be a repeat of the Elsa spectacle." Elsa Knightsbridge, fairy and daughter of the ousted mayor, used a potion to convince Daniel he was in love with her. Thankfully, I was able to stop the elaborate wedding and break her hold on Daniel before the final vows were spoken. I still relived that moment in my nightmares. What if I'd stood there quietly and lost him forever?

Sophie took a turn admiring the ring. "There's zero chance of an Elsa repeat. For one thing, Daniel actually loves you. No love potion required."

"Is this the part where we kiss the ring and promise to do whatever you say?" Millie asked.

I laughed. "I'm not the Godfather." I stroked the diamond with my finger. "But I have decided to refer to it as 'my precious.'"

Millie rolled her eyes. "You're an odd duck."

I flashed a smile. "You're just figuring this out now?"

Lady Weatherby swept into the classroom with her usual regal air. "And what has captured our attention this morning?" She came to peer over my shoulder. "Ah, I see. I heard the news, but wasn't sure whether to believe it. I suppose congratulations are in order."

Suppose? Of course they were!

"It's true," I said. I couldn't wipe the smile from my face even if I wanted to. I was far too happy. The positive energy whirling inside me refused to be contained. "Daniel and I are getting married."

Lady Weatherby's lips formed a tight smile. "The coven wishes you every happiness, Miss Hart. Daniel Starr would not be my choice of husband, of course, but, as they say, there's a ladle for every cauldron. Now, let's get on with our lesson for the day. That is the reason we're gathered here, after all."

Only Lady Weatherby could manage to insult me in the midst of her congratulations. As usual, I took it in stride. I was filled with far too much joy to let a backhanded compliment level me.

The remedial witches settled into their respective chairs as Lady Weatherby took her place at the head of the classroom. "Today's lesson will cover basic wards."

"Ooh, that's a good one," I said, thinking of my office.

Someone had recently snuck in and killed a beloved plant. Althea was chomping at the bit to uncover the culprit.

Lady Weatherby gave me a withering glance. "So glad you approve, Miss Hart."

"Excuse me, Lady Weatherby," Millie interjected, raising her hand.

"Yes, Millie?"

"Before we start, would you mind updating us on the curse?" she asked. "We haven't heard anything about the coven's progress in breaking it since Emma brought back the horn."

Recently, the remedial witches had discovered an old parchment that suggested there was a way to break the curse of the enchantress. A unicorn horn seemed to be a necessary ingredient. I'd used one of the spells on the parchment to summon a sacred unicorn and retrieve its horn. Since then, the coven had been hard at work trying to finish the spell that previous witches had started.

"The coven has its best witches and wizards working on it," Lady Weatherby said vaguely.

"Is that like Prince Humperdinck sending his four fastest ships?" I queried.

The head of the coven gave me a blank look.

Millie groaned. "It's a *Princess Bride* reference. A human world thing."

Lady Weatherby made a dismissive sound.

"It can't be the coven's best witches," Begonia said. "You don't have Laurel working on it, and she was the one who discovered the parchment in the first place."

Lady Weatherby hesitated. "With all due respect, witches, this is the remedial class. The name itself suggests that none of you is the best at any form of witchcraft, eager though you may be."

Ouch. That had to be the harshest thing Lady Weatherby

ever said to us. As the head of the coven, though, she was well within her rights to decide which members she deemed worthy of this Very Important Project. Since the entire fate of the town rested on it, I didn't blame her for being selective.

Millie folded her arms and jutted out her chin, a stubborn look I recognized well by now. "With all due respect to *you*, Lady Weatherby, that's plain offensive. We have proven ourselves time and time again to this coven. Just because we don't tick the right academic boxes doesn't mean we aren't competent witches."

Everyone gaped at Millie. No one openly defied Lady Weatherby, except maybe her mother. And Agnes was safely stowed away in the Spellbound Care Home so opportunities for public humiliation were limited.

To her credit, Lady Weatherby showed great restraint in her response to Millie. "While I agree that you have each shown a certain level of competence outside of this class-room, what we require for this particular project is far more than competence. Surely you can understand that."

No one argued. The silence seemed to give Lady Weatherby pause. "Upon reflection, I think you make an excellent point, Millie." Her gaze rested on Laurel. "Why don't you join our next meeting, Laurel? I suppose there isn't much harm you can do."

Laurel beamed with pride. As the youngest of the reme-dial witches, Laurel showed great promise. "It would be an honor, Lady Weatherby."

Millie sat stony-faced, her hands clasped on the table. She was stewing, I knew it. She intended for all of us to be involved, not just Laurel. Between my engagement and Laurel's selection, we were going to have a hard time boosting Millie's ego this week. Still, it was worth the effort. There was a strong heart beating inside Millie's chest, even though she didn't always show it. I'd glimpsed it often enough to be certain of its existence.

"If we're finished with our little detour, let's move on to wards." Lady Weatherby unhooked her cloak and set it on the back of the chair. "Wards can protect our property, or simply an item of value to us. The consequences for breaching a ward might be benign, such as merely alerting the owner to the breach, or it can yield more drastic results, such as mind-numbing pain to the trespasser."

My head hurt thinking about it. I wouldn't want to inflict pain like that without good reason. I raised my hand. "What if the breach was accidental? Then you've caused pain to an innocent paranormal."

Lady Weatherby looked down her aquiline nose at me. "Then the paranormal will have learned a valuable lesson, will she not?"

My throat tightened. Note to self: steer clear of Lady Weatherby's house.

"We shall begin with simple wards," she continued. "For today's lesson, I would like each of you to design a ward to protect your egg."

I stared blankly at the empty table in front of me. "What egg?"

Lady Weatherby whipped out her wand and, quick as a flash, five eggs appeared on the table, one in front of each of us. "Now spread out in the room so you're not on top of one another. You shall protect these eggs from harm to the best of your ability. Choose whatever ward you think is most appropriate."

I moved to the back of the classroom near the door and began to consider my warding options.

From her spot at the table, Millie waved her hand in the air. "Lady Weatherby, are these eggs hardboiled?"

The head of the coven narrowed her eyes. "No, Millie.

They are not. Why? Were you planning to snack on one after class?"

I suppressed a smile. A joke from Lady Weatherby! Would wonders never cease?

We were given twenty minutes to prepare a ward, then it was time to share our work.

"Now then, witches, are we all confident we've found a way to ward our eggs?" Lady Weatherby asked, and we all nodded. "Good. We'll start with Millie's ward. Sophie, why don't you attempt to breach it?"

Sophie shot a nervous glance at Millie. "You didn't add any mind-numbing pain elements, did you?"

Millie shook her head. "Although I easily could have. Wards are one of my strengths."

"I don't know how you manage to keep track of them all," Lady Weatherby said coolly. "You seem to have so many."

Millie didn't seem to catch her facetious tone. Instead, she took it as a pat on the head and smiled proudly. Bless her.

Sophie lifted a tentative hand toward Millie's egg. A hissing sound filled the air and Sophie jerked back her hand with a muffled "ouch." Sophie quickly stuffed her fingers in her mouth.

"It's just a magical current meant to zap you," Millie said.

"Well, it worked," Sophie said.

Lady Weatherby gave a satisfied nod. "Now yours, Sophie. Millie, you may try to retrieve her egg."

Millie decided to be clever and pointed her wand at the egg. "Don't make me beg/release Sophie's egg." Her wand began to vibrate and then her arm, until her entire body shook. Her wand clattered to the floor.

"Nicely done, Sophie," Lady Weatherby said. "Miss Hart, why don't you attempt to take Laurel's egg?"

I crossed the room to where Laurel's egg rested on the table.

"I'm not sure if Emma is the right one for mine," Laurel said slowly.

"Why should it matter?" Lady Weatherby asked.

Laurel cringed. "Because I've set mine up to…"

As I reached for the egg, a wave of nausea washed over me. There was no way to fight it.

"…cause intense nausea," Laurel finished.

And, with those words, I promptly vomited all over the egg.

Back at the secret lair, we let Millie grumble and grouse about Lady Weatherby's decision to include Laurel in the curse-breaking sessions.

"I mean, we've *all* proven ourselves to be exceptional witches," Millie said. "I don't understand why she can't see that."

"And exactly which coven members are working on it?" Sophie said. "That's what I'd like to know. Are there any specialists? Or is it just the usual suspects like Meg, Ginger, and Professor Holmes?"

"I guess Laurel will be able to tell us after her first meeting," I said.

Laurel nodded emphatically. "Consider me your inside source. I don't care if they swear me to secrecy. You know I'll tell you everything."

Now there was a true friend. The thought led me to my next question. "So, there's something I've been meaning to ask you."

"Yes, we think you should marry him," Millie said, with an annoyed sigh. "Do you really need to rub our noses in it? You've found the perfect guy. A hot angel, no less. Why would you have any doubts?"

I cleared my throat. "As it happens, I don't have any

doubts, but thank you for your insightful commentary. What I want to ask is whether you're all interested in being bridesmaids."

The witches stopped what they were doing and stared at me.

"Really?" Laurel asked. "Even me? Are you sure you don't want me to be a flower girl or something?"

"You're thirteen, not three," I said. "You're an equal member of this group, and as much my friend as everyone else here. I'd be insulted if you weren't a bridesmaid."

Laurel threw her arms around my neck. "You have no idea what it means to hear you say that." As the youngest of five kids in her family, I got the impression that Laurel often felt overlooked and inconsequential, despite her many talents. In our group, she had a place of importance, as everyone deserved.

"Are you going to make us wear hideous dresses?" Millie asked. "That's what brides do, right? Because they want to look the best. They put all the pretty friends in ugly clothes."

Begonia snorted. "I don't think Emma will have any trouble looking beautiful all on her own."

"Thank you, Begonia," I said. "I promise I won't make you wear hideous dresses. In fact, you can come with me to Ready-to-Were and Ricardo will help us all find the perfect dresses."

"That sounds wonderful," Sophie said, clapping her hands. "I've never been a bridesmaid before. This is so exciting."

"Where will you have it?" Millie asked. "The country club?"

I hesitated. "I know it will sound odd to you, but Daniel and I have decided that we'd like the ceremony to take place at Swan Lake."

Begonia's blue eyes widened. "The same place he nearly married Elsa? Isn't that...weird?"

That was the response I expected. "We talked about it and decided that we didn't care. Swan Lake is where we met and it just feels right. Obviously, it will lack the drama that their almost-wedding had, since no one is being forced into marriage this time."

Sophie gave my shoulders a squeeze. "I think it's very romantic. It will be a beautiful wedding, I'm sure of it."

"Have you set the date?" Laurel asked. "Maybe if we manage to break this curse before then, you could actually go on a honeymoon."

I hadn't even considered the possibility. And a honeymoon wouldn't be the only option. I could go home, back to Lemon Grove, Pennsylvania. Not that there was anything there for me now. My whole life was right here in Spellbound, curse or no curse.

"That's a lovely idea," I said. "But let's not get our hopes up." I thought about my biological mother, whether she was still out there somewhere. If we did manage to break the curse ahead of the wedding, maybe I could find her. Maybe she could be here for my big day. The thought was almost too much to bear.

"Emma?" Begonia said gently. "Are you okay?"

I shook off the thoughts. "Yes, sorry. I got caught up thinking about everything there is to do. We've given ourselves six weeks. We figure that's enough time to get our ducks in a row."

Begonia sighed dreamily. "Imagine that. Very shortly, you will be Mrs. Daniel Starr."

I shook my head. "Nope. He will be Mr. Emma Hart."

Millie's mouth dropped open. "You can't be serious."

I laughed. "No, he'll still be Daniel Starr and I'll still be Emma Hart, and we'll be married."

"So which one of us is going to be your maid of honor?" Sophie asked.

I knew this question was coming. Luckily, I'd given it much contemplation before now. "I think there's one para-normal who was born for the role."

Begonia's nose wrinkled in concentration. "Really? Who's that?"

I smiled. "Gareth, of course."

CHAPTER 2

ALTHEA, my Gorgon assistant, sashayed into my office like she was ready to hit the dance floor. The first thing I noticed was the absence of her usual headscarf. Instead, she wore a white linen napkin cinched together with a safety pin.

"Leave something at home today?" I asked and tapped my head.

Althea glanced upward. "The girls and I had a bit of a disagreement this morning. They didn't like what I had to say, so they chewed through the headscarf I was wearing. My other one is in the laundry, so I made due with what I had. It's clean, so don't worry about that."

"You only have two headscarves?" It seemed to me she should have at least five.

"I know," she said. "Silly, isn't it? I should borrow one from my sister, Amanda. She has an entire collection of them."

"Why don't you have a collection?" I asked.

Althea made a face. "I don't *collect* anything. She likes hers with lots of decoration. I prefer the plain ones."

"Well, Amanda is more of a character," I said. The younger

Gorgon made garden gnomes for a living. "Still, it's probably safer to wear a headscarf with pumpkin designs than none at all."

"I'm not going to turn anybody to stone with a napkin," she insisted. "They're well covered. If worse comes to worse, I've got a spell in my dresser at home somewhere that Agnes created for me years ago. It's only a temporary fix, but it would keep me from turning anyone to stone for a limited time."

I smiled at the mention of Agnes. "She designed a spell for you?"

Althea nodded. "Your girl Agnes is full of knowledge and power. I've said a hundred times it's foolish to put that witch out to pasture. Lady Weatherby is talented, but her mother is a force of nature."

I didn't disagree. Then again, I had a soft spot for Agnes and her special brand of crazy.

Althea looked over at the empty windowsill. "Any luck with figuring out who poisoned our plant?"

I followed her gaze. "Not yet. I've been preoccupied with other matters."

"Speaking of other matters," she said, producing a folder. I was so fixated on the diaper-style headscarf, I hadn't even noticed she was holding anything. "You have a new client coming in today."

I pressed my lips together. "Let me guess. The client will be here in half an hour."

Althea winked. "Nope. You've got at least an hour."

I groaned. "Not too serious of an offense, I hope. I'm so distracted by life right now."

"It's a trespassing case," Althea said. "A werelynx called Tomlin."

I scanned the contents of the folder. "Okay, I guess I'd better review this now."

"Is that my cue to run over to Brew-Ha-Ha for a caffeine fix?" she asked.

I smiled. "I think we're getting into a groove." As I flipped the page, Althea's attention was drawn to my hand.

"Stars and stones," she said. "Emphasis on stones. When did you get that fine piece of jewelry, Miss Sparkle?"

I held up my hand for inspection. "I thought you knew. We decided to make it official."

"I wouldn't forget news like that." Althea made a noise of approval. "My, it is *very* official, isn't it? I'd like to have something so official-looking on my finger."

"Nothing is stopping you from buying yourself a beautiful ring," I said.

"I think the paltry salary I get paid might be stopping me," she replied with a pointed look.

"But when you love what you do, it's like you never work a day in your life." I flashed her a cheeky grin.

Althea harrumphed. "That's only what employees say when they don't make a lot of money. Once you marry that wealthy angel of yours, you'll never have to worry about money again."

"It's not like I worry now," I said. "The cost of living isn't very high here." And I'd been given Gareth's house for free. Talk about a leg up in life. Not a day went by that I wasn't grateful.

"I guess Gareth is over the blood moon with all this wedding talk," Althea said.

"That's putting it mildly. I think he knows it's the closest thing to heaven he's ever going to experience." I couldn't help but watch the snakes moving. They were mesmerizing. "I think your girls are staring at me."

Althea glanced down at her ample chest.

"Wrong girls," I said.

"Oh." Althea glanced upward. "That's because they like you."

"Since when?" I asked.

"Trust me. I know when they don't like someone. They're as blunt as I am. Any special request for your latte?" she queried.

I shook my head. "Surprise me."

Althea smiled. "Living on the edge for a change. I like it."

She left the office and I took the little time that I had to review the case file. Tomlin was a thirty-five-year-old were-lynx that had been caught trespassing on the property of Henrietta and Bob Akers. I didn't recognize the address. Tomlin was single and childless. That sounded promising. Maybe he'd be a good candidate for speed dating. It never ceased to surprise me how many single paranormals were roaming around Spellbound.

Tomlin arrived five minutes late and a little disheveled. His shirt was only partially tucked in and his hair looked uncombed. Okay, definitely not a good candidate for speed dating without a makeover.

"You must be Tomlin," I said. "Please come in and have a seat."

Tomlin shuffled in and carefully sat in the chair across from me. He seemed so nervous, I'd need to make a special effort to put him at ease.

Althea bustled in right behind him. "Sorry it took so long. The line was forever because Henrik had a problem with the frother. One of the pixies had to step in with pixie dust."

"Althea, this is Tomlin."

"Nice to meet you. I'm sorry I didn't get you anything," Althea said to Tomlin.

I sipped the latte. I tasted cinnamon and another unfamiliar flavor. "What's the extra shot?"

"I went with Zen," she replied. "You have a lot going on. Zen seemed appropriate."

"You know me so well." As Althea returned to her office, I leaned back in my chair and focused on Tomlin.

"You can relax," I said. "I'm your defense lawyer, not the prosecutor."

He shuddered. "Having a lawyer seems so serious."

"It's kind of serious, but not the end of the world. And it's my job to defend you. If you're going to feel comfortable with anyone during this process, it should be me."

He gave me an anxious smile. "Sorry. Do I seem nervous? I've never been in trouble before. Not officially anyway. I mean, I got in trouble as a kid plenty. Taking extra sweets from the jar and all that. I used to pocket coins I found in my friends' couch cushions."

The werelynx didn't seem to have the confident demeanor often associated with some of the larger shifters. As far as the food chain went, he wasn't too far from the top.

"Why don't you tell me what happened in your own words?" I asked. "Then we can talk about the best options for your case."

Tomlin's knuckles were nearly white from squeezing the arms of the chair. I considered sharing my latte. This guy needed Zen in a major way.

"I didn't realize I was on someone's property," he said. "I thought it was fair game. It wasn't warded or anything."

"Were you within sight of the house?" I asked.

He squinted, thinking. "I could see it, but it wasn't so close that I assumed I was in their yard."

I reviewed the paperwork again. "I don't see any reference to signage. Was there any kind of obvious border?"

Tomlin gave an adamant shake of his head. "No, I wouldn't have been there if I'd seen any indication. I didn't do it on purpose."

"Was this the first time you'd been at this particular spot?"

His gaze drifted to the floor. "No, it was probably my third time."

No wonder the landowners had called Sheriff Astrid. They'd probably given him two free passes already. "Did the owners ever approach you?"

"No, that's the thing. They never approached me at all. I never even saw them. I only knew that I'd done something wrong when the sheriff appeared on my doorstep to arrest me."

That was odd. If they were so upset about it, why didn't they let Tomlin know that he was trespassing? Or hire someone to ward the property? Demetrius had done that for me and I didn't even have the excuse of unwanted visits from a werelynx.

"May I ask what you were doing on their property?" I asked.

Tomlin fidgeted in his seat. "Nothing bad. Looking for vegetables."

"Wouldn't it be easier to go to the market?" I asked.

"I've been teaching myself how to cook and I like to forage. Probably the animal in me," he explained. "My girl-friend...Sorry, my ex-girlfriend was an expert forager, at least for home cooked meals. She always said food tasted better when you took it straight from the land. Geena did all the cooking for us—she's a chef, you see—so when she left me, I had to figure all this stuff out on my own."

"What happened with Geena?" A chef sounded like an ideal partner to me. Delicious meals with no effort from me...yum.

His expression darkened. "She left me for a werefox. Lives across town now. Probably cooks all *his* meals now."

"I bet she did a lot more than cook for you when you lived together," I said. That would explain his disheveled appearance. He was still learning how to take care of himself. At thirty-five years old, I would've hoped for more independence.

"Yeah, Geena did a lot around the house," he said. "She thought I was lazy. That was a running tension in the relationship."

"Would you agree with her assessment?"

He gave me a rueful smile. "I know I was lazy. I let her take control of everything, and I never offered to help. I think she got tired of waiting for me to step up." He paused. "Now I have to step up every day or things don't get done."

Welcome to the real world, I wanted to say. "I'm sorry, Tomlin. This must be a difficult transition for you."

He chewed his fingernail. "I feel like every day is a little better. I'm proud of myself when I learn to do something new. I think this whole experience has boosted my confidence, even though at first I was a complete mess."

"Well, hopefully we can resolve this so that you don't have yet another mess to deal with."

"Thanks," he said. "I've learned my lesson when it comes to foraging. I just wish they hadn't let things escalate. If they'd come to me the first time, we could've avoided this whole thing."

"I totally agree, Tomlin," I said. And now it was my job to find out exactly why.

I sat cross-legged on the bed in the Spellbound Care Home. The common room was being used for arts and crafts, so Agnes and I were working on a manifestation spell in her room. Even though Lady Weatherby was in another curse-breaking meeting, I could tell Agnes was beginning to view that as an excuse not to visit her.

"She always has something more important to do," Agnes grumbled.

"To be fair, breaking the curse is probably more important than anything else she could be doing."

"Fine, Benedict Arnold," she huffed. "Be that way."

"You only know who Benedict Arnold is because I told you," I said.

"See how I apply knowledge I'm given?" Agnes asked. "It'd be nice for you to do the same. I don't understand why these letters are so hard for you to extract. How many times have we tried now?"

Agnes and I had been working to retrieve a packet of letters written by my biological mother. I'd discovered their existence when I was placed under a spell in a lucid dream state and was determined to bring them to Spellbound so I could learn more about my past.

"I stopped counting," I said. "Is it possible that the letters have some kind of protection spell on them in the human world? Something to keep them from being summoned by magic?"

Agnes tapped her long fingernail on her chin. "That's the most intelligent thing I've heard you say...well, ever."

I glared at her. "I'm sure I've said other intelligent things."

"Not to me."

"I challenge you to a game of Scrabble," I said, pointing to the box on her small table by the window. During one of my failed manifestation spells, when I asked for letters, magic misunderstood and brought me Scrabble.

"I don't even understand what that game is," she snapped. "Unless there's drinking involved, how is it fun to spell words?"

"Says the woman who enjoys tiddlywinks," I shot back.

Agnes narrowed her eyes at me in a way that reminded

me of her daughter. "That is a game of pure skill and don't you forget it."

"I'll take your word for it." I uncrossed my legs. "So let's say there's a protective spell on the letters. What can we do to break it?" Without getting hurt, of course.

Agnes thumbed through her pack of tarot cards that she left on the table. "I don't think I've ever had to break a protection spell on an object that was in another realm. Doesn't mean I won't try, of course. I like a challenge as much as any witch."

In truth, Agnes enjoyed a challenge more than most witches. It was one of the qualities that made her behavior so difficult sometimes. Then again, it was also one of the qualities that made her willing to work with me on manifestation spells, no matter how many times I failed.

"This is very interesting," she murmured, studying the cards on the table.

"What is it?" I asked, coming to stand beside her.

"Says right here that I'll be throwing you a wedding shower right here in the care home."

I barked a short laugh. "Where does it say that?"

"Right here," she said, and tapped the card with an image of a sun.

I elbowed her gently. "You're so full of it. Tarot cards can't tell you things like that."

"Are you telling me that you won't let me throw you a shower? I hear they're a big deal in the human world."

"You'd want to do that?" It seemed out of character for Agnes to do something so domestic.

"It's not like I'll ever get to throw one for my own daughter," Agnes said. "You're sort of the next best thing."

"Gee, thanks," I replied sarcastically. I had to admit, though, it was awfully sweet of her. "What makes you think Lady Weatherby will never get married?"

Agnes eyed me curiously. "Do you see any sign of my daughter giving attention to a male? The kind of attention that leads to marriage, I mean."

"She's dedicated to the coven," I said. "I'm sure that takes nearly all of her free time."

Agnes snorted. "You seem to forget that I was the head of the coven once. I certainly made time to find a husband and bear fruit."

"Lady Weatherby is not fruit," I protested. "She's your daughter."

"And stop calling her Lady Weatherby in my presence," Agnes said. "How many times do I need to tell you her name is Jacinda Ruth?"

I patted her shoulder. "She's not my daughter. She's the head of the coven and so, to me, she's Lady Weatherby. I'm sorry if that offends you."

"It doesn't offend me," Agnes said. "It just sounds ridiculous to my ears. I wiped her bottom and rocked her to sleep. She will never be Lady Weatherby to me."

And therein lies the root of their problem. Lady Weatherby wanted respect and her mother refused to give it. I often thought that Lady Weatherby was more to blame for their lack of a relationship, but once in a while, I glimpsed a part of Agnes that reminded me that their relationship is a two-way street.

"So how about it, future Mrs. Cloud Hopper?" Agnes asked. "Do I have your blessing to throw a bridal shower for you?"

What could I say? If nothing else, it would be highly entertaining. "I'd be disappointed if you didn't."

You would think I'd handed Agnes the keys to the castle. Her wrinkled face lit up, making her look a few decades younger. "I'll make all the arrangements. It will be a surprise."

Uh oh. 'Surprise' and 'Agnes' in the same sentence didn't bode well for me.

"Do you need me to give you a list of invitees?" I asked.

She flicked a dismissive bony finger. "The cards will tell me all I need to know."

I didn't love the idea of my bridal shower being based on the whims of Agnes's tarot card collection, but I didn't argue. I could see how happy it made her to do this for me, and I didn't want to disappoint her.

"Okay, slacker," Agnes said. "Break time is over. Let's get back to that manifestation spell. Maybe one of these days you'll actually get the thing you want."

I settled back on the bed and we talked about how to break protection spells in another realm. As always, Agnes proved herself to be more useful than she appeared. Even in Spellbound, residents had a tendency to dismiss the elderly as useless, but I'd spent enough time here to know that these paranormals were full of wisdom and knowledge that could never be replaced. I had no intention of taking her for granted. If there was one thing I'd learned in my short time on earth, it was the simple fact that life was fleeting, even an extended life like hers.

CHAPTER 3

HENRIETTA AND BOB AKERS lived on the closest thing I'd seen to a farm in Spellbound. From what I could tell, they owned about five acres of land with a farmhouse smack dab in the middle. The white clapboard house would have been right at home in Iowa surrounded by cornfields. I parked Sigmund in the driveway and walked up to the front porch to knock on the door. I half expected a dog to come charging out to greet me. Pets aside, though, there was nothing better for a house than a welcoming front porch.

A woman opened the door wearing an apron decorated with daffodils. Her hands were dusted in flour. Everything about her was wiry, including her hair and body.

"Can I help you, miss?" she asked. Her face was lined and weathered, a sure sign of outdoor living.

"I'm Emma Hart," I said. "I'm representing Tomlin Breezeway in the trespassing case, and I'd like to ask you a few questions if you don't mind."

She eyed me suspiciously. "If you're defending that werelynx, should you even be talking to us?"

"You don't have to talk to me," I said. "But I don't see any good reason why you wouldn't. I'm sure you'd like to put this matter behind you as quickly as possible, same as my client."

Henrietta seemed almost as nervous as Tomlin, which was surprising under the circumstances. She wasn't the one charged with a crime.

After a few moments of hesitation, she stepped away from the door to allow me entry. "Bob's in the field right now, but he should be back soon for his snack. We stick to a pretty regular schedule around here."

"I'm the same," I said. "Without a schedule, I'd fall apart." Not to mention Gareth would ridicule me into an early grave.

"How about something cool to drink?" she offered. "I have starmark juice."

"Ooh, I've never had that," I said. "I wouldn't mind trying it, if it isn't too much trouble."

She seemed delighted. "You've never had starmark juice? Well, I'd consider it an honor to be the shifter that introduces it to you."

Although I could tell she was a shifter, I hadn't yet worked out which kind. "You're not a werelynx, too, are you?"

Her beady eyes popped. "Stars and stones, no. Bob and I are wereferrets."

"Like Ricardo," I said brightly.

Henrietta began to relax. "Yes, do you know him? He's a wonderful fella. So fashionable. Bob thinks he looks ridiculous, of course, but I adore his style."

I accepted the glass of juice. "Nobody understands clothes like Ricardo. In fact, he's designing my wedding gown."

Henrietta broke into a wide smile. "You're kidding. That's wonderful. When's the big day?"

"Six weeks to go," I said. "I can't wait."

She sighed happily. "I remember our wedding day like it

was yesterday. Bob and I got married at the Mayor's Mansion, which was highly unusual back then for shifters. You know we tend to do things within our own groups, especially ceremonial events."

I'd learned that not long after I arrived in town, when I investigated the death of a werewolf named Jolene.

"What a coincidence. The Mayor's Mansion is my next stop after this," I said. "I need to speak to Mayor Langtree about my wedding. How long have you been married?"

"Thirty-seven years next month," Henrietta replied.

"That's a long time," I said, impressed. "Tomlin is only thirty-five years old. You've been married longer than he's been alive."

She looked sympathetic. "He's still young? I couldn't tell from the house. My eyesight isn't that good anymore."

We moved from the kitchen to the living room, where I was overwhelmed by pictures on the wall. It seemed like every inch of wall space was covered by the image of a family member's beaming face.

"How many grandkids do you have?" I asked, incredulous.

Henrietta stopped to think. "Is it awful that I've lost track? I think twenty-two."

I whistled. "Holiday dinners must be quite an undertaking."

"Bob and I wouldn't have it any other way. Wereferrets are such a small shifter group. Twenty-two grandkids are a badge of honor."

Henrietta seemed sweet and the pictures on the wall reflected a huge, loving family. It made me feel worse about what they were putting Tomlin through.

"Why didn't you say anything to Tomlin when you saw him in your field?" I asked. "He seems very nice. He didn't know he was on your property. I'm sure if you had just told him…"

Henrietta set down her glass. "You don't understand, Miss Hart. You're not a shifter. Bob and I are wereferrets. We smelled a predator near our home. When we realized it was a werelynx, we got nervous. We're not as young and spry as we used to be. If he chose to attack us, we wouldn't have been able to defend ourselves."

"So this is all because he's a werelynx?" I asked. "If he'd been a wererat or even a pixie, would we be having this conversation?"

"Probably not," Henrietta admitted. She sniffed the air. "I smell Bob. He'll be here any moment."

The front door swung open and Bob appeared in the foyer, looking just as slight and wiry as his wife. "I see we have a visitor."

Henrietta smiled reassuringly at her husband. "Bob, this is Emma Hart. She's defending our trespasser, the werelynx."

"His name is Tomlin," I said quickly. The sooner they could stop viewing him as a predator, the better.

Bob frowned. "Does he say what he wanted from us? Why has he been lurking around our property? We felt like he was stalking prey."

"It isn't what you think at all," I said. "The only thing he was stalking was vegetables for a stew. He's been adjusting to a new lifestyle." I didn't want to divulge the details of his personal life. They seemed too private. "He didn't realize he was on your property. He said if he'd known, he would've left with no problem. He feels terrible about the whole misunderstanding."

"I wanted to go say something to him," Bob said, "but Henrietta wouldn't let me. She thinks I'm too old to defend myself." He shot an accusatory glance at his wife. "Doesn't do much for a wereferret's ego, I'll tell you that much."

"He's only thirty-five," Henrietta said. "I was right to be concerned. He could overtake both of us with no problem."

"Except he wasn't here to overtake you," I said. "He was on the hunt for wild vegetables."

Bob pointed a finger at me. "See? Hunt. You just said it yourself."

I swallowed an exasperated sigh. I could see I had my work cut out for me with these two. Their prejudice against larger shifters ran deep.

"I didn't mean to come and upset you," I said. "I only wanted to ask a few questions so that I could better understand the situation. I get it now. You saw a werelynx three times on your property and believed that he was drawn to the smell of prey. Is that about it?"

Bob shoved his hands in his pockets. "I know that it isn't typical these days for shifters to come after each other. It doesn't mean we don't get nervous, though. We're not in the center of town. If there was trouble out here, we've got no access to magic and no close neighbors to ask for help."

"I understand, Mr. Akers. Thank you for your time." I set my empty glass on a coaster. "The starmark juice was delicious. Thank you for letting me try some."

"My pleasure," Henrietta said. "And if you have any more questions, feel free to come back any time."

"As long as you don't plan to press charges against me for trespassing," I joked.

She rested her hands in her lap. "I don't smell anything on you except goodness, Miss Hart. Bob and I certainly aren't afraid of that."

I banged on the door of the Mayor's Mansion and was intercepted by two large security guards. "Hello there, is Lucy...I mean, Mayor Langtree around?"

"Do you have an appointment?" Tweedledee asked.

"No, but I never have an appointment to see the mayor," I said. "I'm here on personal business."

Tweedledum squinted at me. "So which is it? Personal or business?"

"Personal business," I repeated. "Okay, I can see where you may be confused. It is a matter of a personal nature. Not business at all. Does that help?"

Tweedledum nodded. "Your name?"

I folded my arms. "Seriously? How many times have I been here? It's always you two. Do you really not remember or do you have to pretend so that we don't get too familiar with each other?"

The security guards looked at me blankly.

"Could you just let Lucy know I'm here?" I asked, my impatience growing.

"Yes, Miss Hart," Tweedledee mumbled. The guards disappeared together, and a moment later Lucy's assistant, a young werewolf named Nichole, hurried into the lobby to greet me.

"Many happy returns," she said excitedly. "Can I see your ring? Is that rude to ask?" She grabbed my hand to inspect my finger before I had a chance to respond. "It's amazing. Gosh, I love jewelry. I could wear a ring on every finger and toe. You must be walking on air right now."

"Well, I feel pretty good, but I'm still walking on the ground because that's where I like my feet." Anyone who knew me well knew that the air was the last place I wanted to be. "Is Lucy available?"

"Yes, yes," she said. "Come this way. I was so excited to see the ring. I heard it was stunning and it is. Deacon has done his best work yet. I'm totally using him when the time comes."

Talk about free advertising for Deacon. No wonder he offered such a steep discount.

"Are you dating someone special?" I asked.

She tipped her head back and laughed. "Not yet, but the day will come eventually and I want to be ready."

I didn't have the heart to tell her that the day didn't necessarily come for everyone. Less than a year in Spellbound told me that much. Lots of singles by choice or by virtue of a broken heart. Yet one more reason to be grateful for Daniel.

I followed Nichole to the mayor's office. Although the location in the mansion was the same, Lucy had completely transformed the room. It no longer reminded me of Mayor Knightsbridge. Lucy had removed all traces of the previous mayor. She'd replaced all of the bookcases with artwork and had exchanged the old desk for a pink lacquered desk that reminded me of nail polish.

Lucy fluttered over to hug me. "I'm so glad you're here. I'm sorry I haven't been by to see you. I've been insanely busy." Lucy's fingers brushed against my engagement ring. "I have been desperate to see this fabulous ring."

It dawned on me that I was in dire need of a manicure. I don't think I'd ever shown my hand to so many people in such a short span of time in my entire life. I had no doubt my cuticles were a mess because I'd only recently learned what they were.

Lucy sucked in a breath. "That sparkler is absolutely gorgeous. I cannot imagine a more perfect ring for you."

"Thank you," I said. "Deacon is making our wedding bands, too. We chose simple matching bands with an inscription." Only Daniel and I knew this, but we chose the simple gold bands because they reminded us of halos. We still hoped to one day restore Daniel's good name.

"Can you tell me what the inscriptions will say or are they a secret?" Lucy asked.

"If you live to be a thousand, I want to live to be a thousand minus one day so I never have to live without you," I told her.

"That's so romantic," Lucy said. "And a little long for a ring. I hope it fits! Anyway, I'm thrilled for you. I almost feel like I'm the one who got engaged."

"Thanks, I appreciate it, but I didn't actually come here to show you the ring," I said.

Lucy released my hand. "No?"

"It is related to the wedding, though," I said. "Daniel and I discussed it, and we're hoping that you'll agree to officiate the ceremony." I held my breath and waited anxiously for her response.

Lucy appeared stunned. For a moment, I thought she might decline, until she let out a shriek of pure joy. The sound echoed in the office and likely reverberated throughout the entire mansion. She squeezed my body against hers and planted a wet kiss on my cheek.

Tweedledee and Tweedledum appeared in the doorway, summoned by her shriek.

"Everything okay, Madame Mayor?" Tweedledee inquired.

She swatted them away. "I'm fine, Bertram. I got overly excited by Emma's question."

Bertram? I resisted the urge to laugh.

"Yes, ma'am," Bertram said. "Sorry to interrupt." The guards disappeared as quickly and quietly as they'd arrived. Lucy turned her attention back to me.

"Are you nuts?" she asked. "Do you really think you need to ask? I'm out of my mind with excitement. This is the best question you could possibly have asked me."

I was relieved to hear how pleased she was. I found it difficult to gauge how certain friends would react to my request. I'd worried that Lucy would rather be a bridesmaid. Glad to know that wasn't the case.

"Give my assistant the date and we'll put it straight onto the calendar," Lucy said, back in business mode. "And make sure whoever is throwing your shower and bachelorette party send a message to my assistant. I'll need to block those days as well."

I saluted her. "Aye, aye, Captain Mayor."

"Please tell me you have not gone to Ricardo for a dress yet," Lucy said. "You know I need to be involved in that."

"I have not gone yet, and yes, you will absolutely be my number one shopping companion."

Lucy's wings fluttered furiously. That was how I knew she was truly excited. "This wedding will erase Elsa Knightsbridge from everyone's memory," Lucy said. "And, this time, the guests will make it to the reception. We'll deserve a good meal after sitting through two sets of Daniel's vows."

"Our vows will be better," I said. "Promise."

She twirled around me, giddy with happiness. "Oh, Emma. It's going to be the *most* perfect day. Just you wait and see."

From her lips to the gods' ears.

CHAPTER 4

WHEN I ARRIVED at my therapy appointment, Dr. Hall wasted no time grilling me about my upcoming nuptials. She had zero interest in the ring. Instead, she was hyperfocused on the ceremony.

"What do you mean you don't want to take a blood vow? It's a wedding!" She blinked at me in disbelief.

From my place on the therapist's sofa, I took a hesitant sip of my drink, a new cocktail called Crimson Rush that Dr. Hall referred to as 'delightful.'

"I'm not a vampire and neither is Daniel," I said. "Why would we do blood vows?"

She devoured the liquid in her glass like it was actual blood. "Because it's the done thing, darling. The real question is—why wouldn't you?" She leaned back in her chair and awaited my insightful response.

"Maybe I don't want to risk red stains on my white wedding dress?" I mused. "Or maybe it's plain gross?"

"Bite your tongue," Catherine admonished me. "No, seriously. Bite your tongue. You might draw blood." Her fangs poked out just enough to remind me why she was so enthusiastic about blood.

"Stop," I said. "You're supposed to calm me, but you're freaking me out."

Catherine cocked her head. "I'm supposed to calm you?" She threw her head back and a deep, throaty laugh escaped her. "My darling Emma, when have I ever calmed you?"

True enough. Catherine wasn't exactly the warm, fuzzy therapist I'd expected to have. That was apparently Thalia's domain, her therapy competition. Still, I enjoyed our sessions and was grateful to have an impartial ear. Catherine's best quality was that she didn't sugarcoat things—she got right to the marrow of a situation and sucked it out. I shivered. It was probably best not to equate my vampire therapist with sucking anything—the thought was too disturbing.

"You've been a big help to me," I said.

Catherine's expression softened for a brief moment. "Well, don't let word get around. I don't need to be as busy as Thalia. That muse is too devoted to her clients. She has no life of her own."

"I hear she has no bar either, not in her office anyway." Although it was unorthodox, the weekly cocktails seemed to have the desired effect.

"Bah! A bar?" Catherine scoffed. "She needs a nursery in her office. She's too busy dedicating herself to crybabies."

I smiled. "Is that what I am to you? A crybaby?"

She went behind the bar and poured herself another drink. "Sometimes. Mostly not, though."

"Fair enough," I replied. As always, Catherine held no punches.

"So what's the latest on the search for your crazy mom?" she asked.

My head jerked toward her. "My crazy mom? Why would you say a thing like that?"

She maintained a poker face. "Because she gave you up. Clearly she's nuts."

I sat up straighter. "That's a horrible thing to say. We don't know what her reasons were. She obviously wanted to keep me, but circumstances forced her to send me to safety."

"Oh, so you're Moses in the basket now, are you? Being sent up the river? Way to inflate your importance."

I gaped at her. "Okay, sometimes I really do question your methods."

"Need I remind you that I have a degree from an accredited vampire university," she replied coolly. "My methods are sound."

I ignored her lame attempt at a defense. "My biological mother wrote me letters that my parents hid from me. In my dream, my mom was upset when my biological mom came to see me. She said that her visit endangered me. Then my mom died under suspicious circumstances. I don't think I'm over-reaching to suggest that I was given up for my own safety."

Catherine tapped on her glass. "I honestly hope you're right, Emma." Her usual cold tone thawed. "But you need to remember that not all reunions are happy ones. Even if you manage to manifest these letters, they may not say what you want them to say. Are you prepared for that?"

My hands fidgeted. "Truthfully? Probably not."

"And what do you imagine the letters to say?"

Did I want to admit the truth out loud? I drew a deep breath and decided to go for it. "That she loves me. That she didn't want to give me up, but she had no choice. That if she had to do it all over again, she'd make a different choice."

"But then you never would have met your parents," Catherine pointed out. "Would you trade those relationships for a woman you don't even know?"

A good question. I loved my parents with every fiber of my being and now I felt guilty for wishing them away.

"No," I said in a quiet voice. "You're right. I wouldn't trade them for anyone. I guess I just want to know my biological parents. Who they are and why they left me. That's all."

"And what if the letters don't say what you want? What if your mother was simply checking on your welfare out of guilt, not love?"

I shifted uncomfortably. "I suppose that would be better than complete disinterest."

Catherine leaned forward and peered at me. "Is that what you ultimately hope to get out of these letters? To know that she cared?"

"I don't know. Sometimes I feel like I want more than that," I said. "I lost my mother at a young age, so I guess I feel like I've missed out twice."

"You're overthinking it," Catherine said. "You need to get back to basics. Deep down, everyone wants the same thing. We just don't necessarily acknowledge it."

"What's that?" I asked.

"We want to know that during our time here, someone in the world loved us."

I said nothing.

Catherine drained her glass dry and set it on a nearby coaster. "Have I ever told you the story about my cousin, Elena?"

"The one that refused to marry?"

Catherine nodded. "So you do pay attention when I speak. She was beautiful and had many offers, but she refused them all."

"Because she was a feminist ahead of her time?" I asked.

"No, because she fell in love with a prince who was already married to someone else."

34

I smiled. "Sounds like an upside down fairy tale. What does it have to do with me?"

Catherine held up a finger, her signal for patience. "Elena met Kristoff in the woods one day. They were both fans of archery. Of course, Elena did hers in secret because she was a woman. When she first met Kristoff, she didn't know he was a prince."

"They fell in love shooting arrows?" I asked. Not the most romantic activity in the world unless you were Cupid.

"They fell in love doing something they both enjoyed," Catherine corrected me. "For months they met in the woods and Kristoff told her all about his life in the castle."

"Including his wife?" I asked.

Catherine pretended to zip her lips. "He didn't like to speak of her, only to say that he was forced to marry at a young age because of his title and that there was no love between them."

I could see where this was going. "But he wouldn't leave the princess."

"Nor did he want to leave Elena. It was a hopeless situation, as these things often are."

That had to be the most sympathetic statement Catherine had ever uttered.

"So what happened?" I prodded.

"Kristoff couldn't handle the guilt of loving another, so they decided to stop seeing each other so often," she explained. "It was too difficult for both of them. They always left each meeting wanting more. So, instead, they made a pact to only see each other when the moon was full. They would meet for an hour in the woods with their bows and arrows in complete silence."

"They didn't talk at all?"

"Not a word. They decided it was best so that neither was tempted to say something too tender or affectionate. They only wanted to be in each other's company and feel the love they shared."

"That seems unfair to Elena," I said. "She never had the chance to meet anyone else because she was still in love with Kristoff. He should have let her go."

"But don't you see? As limited as it was, that relationship was enough for her. She recognized that she'd never love anyone the way she loved Kristoff, so she decided that their connection was enough to sustain her in this world."

"But you told me before that she died alone," I objected.

"She died without a husband, but she wasn't alone," Catherine said. "She had love. She just didn't have it in the socially acceptable way."

"During her time here, she knew someone loved her and she loved him," I murmured. "And that was enough."

Catherine lifted my glass to her mouth and finished it without asking. Then she smacked her lips together and said, "Exactly."

"I hear congratulations are in order," Sheriff Astrid said. The blond Valkyrie strode into my office and stretched out in the chair in front of me. Her long legs reached the feet of my desk. "Dazzle me, Hart."

I flashed the ring. "Deacon did an amazing job. It's exactly the way Daniel and I described it to him."

"Let's hope your wedding is far less eventful than his last one."

"I have every confidence ours will go off without a hitch." The more I said it, the more I hoped to convince myself. My life had a way of throwing one curveball after another. Bobbing and weaving seemed to be the key to my survival.

"I call dibs on your bachelorette party," Astrid said. "Britta and I will plan a night for everyone to remember." She laughed. "Or possibly to forget, depending on how the night goes."

"I'll leave it in your capable hands," I said. "As long as there are no strippers." Did Spellbound even have strippers? I certainly hadn't met any yet.

A tapping on the windowpane grabbed our attention.

"Sedgwick?" I squinted. No, it wasn't my cantankerous owl.

"That's the owl from my office," Astrid said, grimacing. "This can't be good news."

I walked over to the window and opened it. I took the scrawled note from the owl's foot and handed it to Astrid. It was so odd to have an owl fly off without a word. I'd definitely become accustomed to Sedgwick's snappy comebacks.

Astrid's brow creased. "Sweet Odin's ravens. I've got to run. There's a dead body over in the Enchanted Woods section of town."

Ugh. "Anything I can help with? I was just finishing up here for the evening."

Astrid didn't hesitate. "If you're sure. It'll be faster than waiting for Britta. Besides, she's probably already down at the Horned Owl for the evening. Her idea of happy hour seems to encompass an entire evening."

"Can't blame a girl for wanting to have fun," I said. "Is she meeting Paisley there?"

Astrid shrugged. "No clue. I can't seem to keep up with my sister."

We drove in the sheriff's jalopy to the Enchanted Woods. When we arrived in front of the house, I was startled to recognize the figure waiting on the front lawn.

"What's Tomlin doing here?" I asked.

"You know him?"

"I'm defending him in a trespassing case," I replied.

As we crossed the front lawn, Tomlin seemed surprised to see me as well. "Miss Hart. Good evening, Sheriff."

"Are you the one that alerted my office?" Astrid asked.

"Yes. Seamus is my neighbor," the werelynx said, visibly upset. "I found him on the floor of the kitchen. He was still alive when I got here, but he couldn't speak. It was like all his muscles gave out." Tomlin squeezed his eyes closed, as though trying to block the image from his memory. "By the gods, it was awful."

"Can you show us where he is?" Astrid asked.

We followed Tomlin inside the house to where the pixie lay on the floor. He was contorted, as though he'd lost control of his body. His wings were crushed and his eyes were still open, staring into the void.

"Do you often come in and out of his house if he doesn't answer the door?" Astrid asked.

"No, but I was here earlier and had to run home," Tomlin said. "When I came back to see how he liked his dinner, I found him on the floor." His voice drifted off as the image resurfaced.

"Is that typical for you?" I asked, perplexed. "To see how he enjoyed his dinner?"

"No," Tomlin said. "But I made the stew. I wanted to make sure it wasn't awful. I'm still not very good at the whole cooking thing."

Astrid scrutinized the disheveled werelynx. "Why did you make dinner for your neighbor if you're not good at it?"

"He's been teaching himself to cook," I said, instinctively rising to my client's defense.

Tomlin raked a hand through his hair. "Seamus and I had argued recently. It was my peace offering. Dear gods, what if he choked on a carrot? What if this is my fault?"

Astrid placed a comforting hand on the werelynx's arm. "I

know it's hard, but try to stay focused, Tomlin. Tell me what the two of you argued about."

Tomlin glanced sadly at the pixie. "Does it matter now?"

"It might," Astrid said. "There's a dead pixie on the floor and we need all the help we can get."

Tomlin swallowed hard. "It's not murder if he choked on a carrot, right?"

I needed to get him back on track. "Did he seem okay when you dropped off his dinner?"

Tomlin nodded quickly, his eyes wide with fear. "Perfectly fine. We chatted and he thanked me for the stew. We joked about our bachelor lifestyles. How much we hated doing everything for ourselves."

"You didn't see anyone else stop by the house?" Astrid asked.

"No," Tomlin replied, "but I wouldn't necessarily hear anyone over here if I wasn't paying attention."

"Do you know if Seamus had problems with anyone else?" I asked. "Maybe someone he didn't resolve an issue with over a pot of stew?"

He snapped his fingers. "He mentioned that a buddy had loaned him money. Maxwell. There was some disagreement over payment."

"Maxwell? You mean the leprechaun that works at the Shamrock Casino?" Astrid asked.

"You know him?" Tomlin asked.

Astrid nodded. "He's friendly with Britta, my sister. She spends a lot of time there."

"I'm surprised she and Phoebe don't know each other better," I remarked. Phoebe Minor was my friendly neighborhood harpy and she excelled at gambling almost as much as she excelled at belittling others. Hers was a true gift.

The front door opened and Astrid's team came in with a

floating stretcher to take the pixie's body away for an autopsy.

"Be careful not to touch anything," Astrid said firmly. "Don't contaminate the scene."

"Should I go?" Tomlin asked, watching as his neighbor was lifted onto the hovering stretcher. When someone closed Seamus's eyes, Tomlin winced.

"Let's talk outside," Astrid said, and the three of us vacated the kitchen. She seemed to sense Tomlin's discomfort as well. It couldn't be easy for him. He'd just witnessed the death of his neighbor and friend.

Once we were a reasonable distance from the house, Astrid fixed Tomlin with her hard stare. "Now tell us why you were arguing."

Tomlin made a halfhearted attempted to tuck in his shirt. "It was over a tree," he said.

"Which tree?" Astrid asked.

Tomlin pointed upward. "The one we're standing underneath."

Astrid and I both glanced skyward. The tree was fairly large with a thick trunk and dozens of leafy branches.

"What's wrong with the tree?" I asked. It seemed perfectly healthy.

"Nothing's wrong with it," Tomlin said. "That's the problem. It keeps growing, to the point where half the branches were hanging over the fence into my yard. The leaves were making a mess. I have enough mess in my life. I don't want any that I'm not responsible for."

I walked over to the adjoining fence and peered up at the tree. "There are branches missing on this side."

Tomlin lowered his head. "That's because I took the liberty of trimming them."

"Trimmed them?" Astrid repeated. "You cut them off completely."

Tomlin turned beet red. "I asked him repeatedly to trim them so they weren't encroaching on my property, but he refused," he explained. "I was forced to take matters into my own hands."

"Did he say why?" I asked. It wouldn't have surprised me to learn the tree was incredibly rare and protected under an environmental ordinance. Spellbound was full of bureaucratic red tape.

"Because his mother planted the tree and she's gone now, so he didn't want to change it," Tomlin said. "He and his brother grew up playing under this tree. Apparently, it was like I decimated his happy childhood memories."

Astrid rubbed her chin. "I can see why he was upset over it."

"Me, too," I replied. "Emotional attachments can be quite strong, even to trees."

"When he initially refused, I thought he was being stubborn. Afterward, when he explained his feelings, I understood," Tomlin said. "By then it was too late, though. Boy, was he upset when he saw those missing branches." Tomlin shook his head. "I'd never seen him like that. Seamus was always so easygoing."

I didn't blame the pixie. Seamus had a strong attachment to the tree because of his dead mother. I wasn't prone to anger either, but even I would've been upset over such a violation.

"When did you mend fences?" I asked. "Today when you brought over dinner?"

Tomlin placed a steadying hand on the trunk of the tree. He still seemed distraught over Seamus, which was completely understandable.

"No," he said. "We talked a few days ago after not speaking for a week. That's why the stew was a peace offering. We'd both had time to reflect."

"Is that what happened when you cut down the branches?" Astrid asked. "He stopped talking to you?"

Tomlin dug a toe in the dirt. "Not exactly. He yelled at me first, but I locked the door and wouldn't let him in the house. I wasn't sure what he would do. His head looked ready to explode and his wings were fluttering angrily." He shook his head. "You don't want to see a pixie when he's pissed."

"Then you probably shouldn't cut down his tree branches," Astrid remarked.

"I was sorry, okay?" Tomlin blurted out. "We got into a small war with each other. He would leave rotten eggs on my front porch and hide them so I had to find them in order to get rid of them."

Astrid stifled a laugh. "Very mature."

Tomlin shrugged. "This is what happens when two guys who aren't fighters get into a tussle."

"Did you escalate matters after the rotten eggs?" I asked.

Tomlin pursed his lips. "I may have replaced his pixie dust with ground coffee."

"Not very magical," Astrid murmured.

"Coffee?" I said. "It is for me."

Beads of sweat appeared on Tomlin's forehead. "The bottom line is we resolved the dispute. Everything was fine. Tonight was meant to seal the deal."

Astrid watched as her team drove off with the pixie's body. "I hate to say it, Tomlin, but the only thing tonight sealed was his fate."

CHAPTER 5

AFTER A MORNING OF ACADEMY CLASSES, I waltzed into the future home of Begonia's business, Spelled Ink. Thanks to an academy assignment, Begonia discovered a talent for magical tattoos that she decided to monetize. Her boyfriend, the sexy vampire Demetrius Hunt, surprised her by agreeing to bankroll the business.

Begonia and Demetrius stood in the middle of the empty room, discussing plans for the interior with a leggy blonde. Instinctively, I glanced at Demetrius to see if his gaze stayed where it belonged and I was relieved to see that it did. Even better, he looked at Begonia with a mixture of adoration and respect. Like Daniel, his womanizing days seemed to be over.

"Emma, you're here," Begonia said happily. "I'd like you to meet our interior designer, Hayley."

When Hayley turned toward me, I nearly had to shut my eyes. Talk about blinded by beauty.

"You're a muse," I said. There was no doubt in my mind. "I thought Thalia was the only one in town." Thalia was Dr. Hall's therapist archenemy.

"She's definitely not the only one." Hayley flipped her

corn-silk hair over her shoulder. "I don't do therapy, though. My focus is on interior design. *That's* my calling in life." She bestowed a megawatt smile upon Begonia. "And creating beautiful body art just might be Begonia's."

My friend beamed like she'd been granted eternal youth. "Markos has worked with Hayley on other projects," Begonia said. Markos was the most successful architect in town as well as its only minotaur. "He's the one that suggested her services."

"I ran into Markos at Petals last week," Demetrius explained. "When I told him about Spelled Ink, he thought Hayley would be perfect for the job."

"You and Markos were both in Petals?" I queried.

Demetrius flashed a smile, revealing his impressive fangs. "I stopped by to pick up flowers for Begonia, and Markos happened to be there choosing flowers for his office manager for Administrative Assistant Appreciation Day."

Gulp. There was a day when I was supposed to show Althea I appreciated her? Part of me was surprised she didn't make a fuss about it. As usual, I was clueless.

"But she's his office manager, not his assistant," Begonia pointed out.

Demetrius shrugged. "Maybe he wanted an excuse to buy her flowers. Have you seen Beatrice? It's easy to understand."

Beatrice, I sighed inwardly. The pretty witch was no fan of mine. She was convinced Markos still had a thing for me, despite my relationship with Daniel. The visit to Petals was encouraging, though. It suggested that maybe Markos had finally moved on.

"You should hear Hayley's vision for my office," Begonia said. "I can hardly wait to see the results."

"I'm sure it's going to be wonderful," I said.

"It will be, thanks to Demetrius," Begonia said, casting a shy look at her fanged paramour.

"Not *all* thanks to me," the vampire replied. "If it weren't for your talent, this whole endeavor would be pointless." He gave her a quick kiss on the cheek and Begonia's cheeks burned crimson. Stars and stones, they were the sweetest couple I'd ever seen. We definitely ended up with the right partners, not that I had any doubt.

"How long until you're operational?" I asked.

"It will be a while," Begonia said. "I want everything to be perfect before we start bringing in customers. Best foot forward, right?"

"Right," I agreed. "And you've got to get to work designing more magical tattoos."

"I'll be first in line," Hayley said. "I absolutely fell in love with the idea. The designs are exquisite."

"Hayley's given me more ideas for tattoos," Begonia added. "She's a fountain of creativity."

Hayley winked. "That's a muse for you. Always infusing others with ideas."

"What an amazing skill," I said. Drop-dead gorgeous with the ability to inspire and help others achieve their dreams. If I could choose to be any paranormal, a muse seemed like a pretty good deal to me.

"Everyone has the potential to act as a muse for another," Hayley said. "It's simply a matter of giving that much of yourself to another. To share insight and true thoughts can make one vulnerable. It's not as easy as it sounds."

"Sounds like a relationship," I said.

"It is a very special kind of relationship," Hayley said. "Built on absolute trust."

A smile touched my lips. "So Daniel could be my muse?"

"Very likely. And you could be his," Hayley replied.

Begonia wrapped her arms around Demetrius's firm waist. "Dem is definitely mine. If it weren't for him, I never would have taken Spelled Ink this far."

He hugged her tightly. "Don't be ridiculous. This venture would have happened with or without me. As much as I'd love to take credit for inspiring you, Spelled Ink is entirely your creation."

Begonia grew flushed. "It is, isn't it?"

Demetrius gave her an affectionate kiss on the cheek. "Do you know I don't think I've ever had a partnership with a woman before? All the years I've been undead...It's shameful, really."

"Not to me," Begonia said. "I'm glad I was the first."

"While we're on the subject of partnerships," Demetrius said, "when can Begonia and I take you and Daniel out for dinner? We want to celebrate the happy occasion."

My brain went into overdrive searching for an excuse. I knew Daniel wouldn't be enthusiastic to spend an evening out with the vampire. He tolerated Demetrius for my sake, but he preferred to keep the hotness at arm's length.

"I'll check our schedules," I said. "It's so busy right now, you know. The big day is weeks away and still so much to do."

"If you need any help, I can recommend a wedding muse," Hayley said.

I waved her off. "I'll be fine, thanks. If you know a muse who can add a few more hours to the day, though, that would be perfect."

Hayley laughed. "I think we can all use one of those."

I tapped an imaginary watch on my wrist. "And no surprise that my time here is up. Sorry, Begonia, but I've got to run to meet Daniel to look at wedding venues, then I'm off to the casino."

"That sounds fun," Begonia said.

"It would be, if Astrid and I weren't going to interview a suspect. The autopsy report showed that Seamus died from hemlock poisoning, so it's officially a murder investigation."

Astrid's owl had delivered the message this morning on my way to the academy. To say I was surprised was an understatement.

Demetrius wore a grim expression. "Is that the pixie over in the Enchanted Woods? I heard he choked on a carrot."

"Apparently not." I gave Begonia a quick peck on the cheek. "I'll let you know about dinner."

I left the building and began to run, not wanting to be late for Daniel. For once, I actually wished I had my broom.

That night Astrid and I met at Shamrock Casino to talk to Maxwell, the leprechaun who'd loaned money to Seamus. No surprise that Maxwell worked at the casino. It seemed that every leprechaun in town had a stake in the gambling business the same way all the vampires seemed to own a stake in the Blood Bank cooperative.

We located Maxwell at a card table in the back of the room. It was the middle of a shift and he was busy dealing to five customers.

Astrid cracked her knuckles. "I'm so anxious to play, but I know I can't right now."

"Yes," I agreed. "Probably not the best time to lose money when you're on official duty."

She shot me a horrified glance. "Who says I would lose money? You seem to forget how often I kick your butt at poker."

I smiled. "Not as often as Lucy."

Astrid rolled her eyes. "You got me there. That fairy has a gambling gene. I can't compete with her skills."

"I think it's more her competitive nature. She'd gather more souls than you on the battlefield even though she's not the Valkyrie," I said.

"I'm not so sure about that," Astrid said.

The sheriff flashed her badge and signaled to get Maxwell's attention. A replacement dealer was quickly brought in so he could take a break. In his green waistcoat and tiny black hat, he was the quintessential leprechaun.

"With that shiny badge, I take it you're not here to play, ladies," he said, approaching us.

"Unfortunately not," Astrid said. "Official business only. Is there somewhere private we can talk?"

Maxwell beckoned us to the employee break room. It was nearly as loud and busy in there as in the casino itself. The leprechauns were a lively bunch, each one telling a story with more animation and humor than the last. We sat at a bistro table in the back corner of the room for as much privacy as possible.

"This is about dearly departed Seamus, isn't it?" he said, his expression somber. "I heard the news from a customer."

"Seamus was a friend of yours, wasn't he?" Astrid asked.

Maxwell nodded somberly. "Good friends. We go back years. We were both the wee lads in our class at school. We looked ridiculous sitting between these hulking werewolves and trolls. Seemed only natural to become friends."

The pixie and the leprechaun. It sounded like a good fable. Or a bar joke. "We understand you had a falling-out with your good friend, Seamus," I said.

Maxwell appeared contrite. "It all seems silly now. I was so angry about the money. Who cares about money, right? You can't take it with you." His face soured. "Can't take anything with you except your dignity, and even that fails sometimes."

"Can you tell us more about the dispute?" Astrid asked. "We were told he owed you money?"

Maxwell blew out a breath. "Yeah. I loaned him a bag of coins last year, after his girlfriend left him. He needed money to pay her half of the living expenses those first few months.

Their budget had been tight with him between jobs and her leaving put him in a bad spot financially."

"Did he ask you for money or did you offer?" I asked.

"I offered," Maxwell replied. "It never would have occurred to Seamus to ask."

"So what happened?" Astrid asked. "He decided not to pay you back?"

Maxwell covered his pink cheeks with his hands. "That's probably how I made it seem to him, that he decided not to pay me back. He was trying to find a decent job—a job that paid enough so that he could afford to stay. He was desperate not to move, and I didn't blame him. It had been his mother's house before she died and he was very attached to it. His life was turned upside down when Leanne left him. I didn't want to make it worse by demanding the money back."

I frowned. "If you were sympathetic, why were you upset about his failure to pay you back?"

Maxwell flicked a bit of lint from his sleeve. "Part of me felt like it was tough love," he said. "That I was being the friend he needed. He'd been wallowing in self-pity for months. I wanted him to snap out of it. I began to think the only way I could do that successfully was to force his hand. I figured if I took drastic action, it might motivate him to make the changes he needed to make."

I began to feel sorry for Maxwell. It did seem like he was trying to be a good friend, even though it wasn't exactly the way I would've gone about it. He clearly regretted it now.

"Did you ever confront him about the loan?" Astrid asked.

"We had one argument about the money," Maxwell said. "It was here, actually. I even got in trouble for it because customers overheard us. I was feeling worked up that night because Leanne had come in with her husband and Seamus had seen them. I was upset for him. I worried that he'd go further down the shame spiral. I guess I overreacted." He closed his eyes, full of regret. "I should have been more supportive. It was dumb to think I could make him heal faster by withdrawing my friendship. He was down and I kicked him. Hard."

"I'm sorry, Maxwell," I said. "Your heart was in the right place."

"Do you know why we're talking to you about this?" Astrid asked.

Maxwell rubbed his ear. "Now that you mention it, I don't. You don't normally go around asking questions about someone unless the death is suspicious, right?"

Sheriff Astrid nodded sagely. "That's right. It's an active murder investigation."

Maxwell blinked. "But I heard he choked on a carrot or something. How is that murder?"

"It's murder when the victim ingests hemlock," I said. "Seamus didn't choke, Maxwell. He was poisoned."

Maxwell sank deeper into his chair. Either he had the best poker face I'd ever seen or he was truly shocked by the revelation. "Hemlock? Why on earth would anyone poison a pixie like Seamus? He was harmless, a bit sad even."

I offered him a sympathetic smile. "That's what we're here to find out, Maxwell. Is there anything you can think of that would be helpful for the investigation? Anyone else he may have been at odds with?"

Maxwell shrugged his tiny shoulders. "The only name that springs to mind is Leanne, but I don't see why she would have an axe to grind with him. She was the one who left him to rot."

"What about Leanne's husband?" Astrid asked. "Is there any reason to think that he'd wish Seamus harm?"

Maxwell's brow wrinkled. "Now that you say that, Seamus and Leanne did have a moment together the night I saw them here. I thought she was just being nice, but maybe there was more to it than that and her husband didn't like it."

"When you say they had a moment," I began, "what do you mean by that?"

Maxwell rubbed his ear again. I recognized it as his thinking gesture. How about that? Even dealers had a tell. "They talked in private over by the slot machine. I saw her hug him and kiss him on the cheek. I assumed she was only trying to cheer him up because he'd been such a sad sack, but who knows?"

"And Leanne's husband saw them, too?" Astrid asked.

Maxwell nodded. "Oh, yeah. It was very awkward for us when we saw them come in. The guy's so different from Seamus. Uptight and dull as a dwarf."

"Maybe that's exactly what attracted Leanne to him," I said.

Maxwell adjusted his crooked vest. "Could be. Wouldn't surprise me that Seamus was too laid-back for her." He heaved a sigh. "I say that like it didn't bother me, of course, but I'm the one that decided to go the tough love route and lost my best friend." He paused and closed his eyes. "Forever."

I gave his hand a gentle pat. "I'm sure deep down Seamus knew what you were up to and that your intentions were good. I know it's hard, but try not to beat yourself up."

"We should all get to roll the dice one more time," he said. "It's the least we deserve."

I didn't disagree.

CHAPTER 6

READY-TO-WERE WAS my favorite clothing boutique in Spellbound and there was no one I trusted more to make me look good on my wedding day than Ricardo. The wereferret had a magical sense of fashion that nobody could duplicate. Lucy was the only one that came close and she had the excuse of being a fairy.

"It is my most favorite bride in Spellbound. Come in! Come in!" Ricardo pounced on us before we had a chance to fully enter the shop. He was decked out today in skinny lemon-yellow trousers, a black T-shirt, and a colorful striped scarf. Only a beret and a baguette were missing from the ensemble.

"Thank you for spending the afternoon with us," I said. "I know it's going to be a lot of work."

"Ah, but it is the best kind of work." He gave me a kiss on each cheek before he moved on to Lucy and my coterie of bridesmaids. "I see you brought your fashion sergeant with you."

"Fashion mayor," Lucy corrected him. "And I'm here for

moral support. I'll only step in if I truly believe a fashion crime is being committed."

"Sounds reasonable to me," Ricardo said. He ushered us further into the shop so we could fan out. "I've taken the liberty of pulling a selection of dresses I think you will adore. Bridal on the left. Bridesmaids on the right. Enjoy!"

I directed the remedial witches to the right, while Lucy and I dug through the dresses on the left. To my surprise, they weren't all white. He'd tossed in peach, cream, and even a salmon pink.

"That one is in case you are feeling sassy," he said, when he noticed my gaze pinned on the salmon pink.

"I love it," Lucy screeched, fluttering over to investigate. "I'd definitely go for this one."

"Given that Elsa was a pink freak, I think it's best that I steer clear," I said.

Lucy's lips puckered. "Good point."

"I have segmented them by color and levels of fancy," Ricardo said. "Most of the options here are lower on the fancy scale because…well, it's you, Emma."

"I don't consider it an insult," I said, smiling at him. "I'm not a fancy pants. Never have been." Never had the opportunity to be fancy back in Lemon Grove. Shopping here was still a real luxury as far as I was concerned and I appreciated every second of it.

"What about this one?" Lucy asked, lifting a hanger off the rack. The white dress was plain at the top with lace sleeves and lace trim at the bottom.

"It's pretty, but I'm not a lace person," I said. "It reminds me of my grandmother's doilies."

"What's a doily?" Lucy asked.

"She used them on tabletops to keep the wood from getting scratched, I think," I said. "Anyway, they were made of white lace, so that's what I think of."

"Are you thinking floor-length or shorter?" Ricardo asked. "Personally, if I had your legs, I would be showing them off on my wedding day."

"Thanks, but a micro-mini bridal dress isn't my style," I said. "Daniel might think I'm under a spell."

"We need a dress that screams 'happiness,'" Lucy said. "Show us happiness, Ricardo."

He raised a finger. "That I can do." He plucked a hanger from the far end and displayed a long white dress. It reminded me of a dress Elizabeth Bennet from *Pride and Prejudice* would wear. It was high-waisted in the Empire style with capped sleeves and a long, straight skirt.

Lucy drew in a breath. "Great glitter balls. It's perfect for you. That low, square neckline will be lovely with your long neck."

"And it has a narrow waist like you," Ricardo said. He thrust the dress into my hands. "Try it on. Let us all marvel at your beauty."

I wasn't sure about the marveling part, but I went into the fitting room to get changed. I never tired of the magic involved in Ricardo's clothing. It didn't matter what size dress I brought in with me. Once I slid it over my head, the dress changed shape to match mine. That was the great thing about using pixies and fairies as seamstresses. I'd still need fittings to make sure my shape didn't change between now and the wedding (fingers crossed), but weight loss or gain was a much easier fix with magic.

My breathing hitched when I looked at myself in the mirror. I looked like a real bride. All that was missing was a floral wreath on my head. I wasn't a fan of veils and had already decided on the headdress. Begonia had tried to talk me into a twisted antler headdress like Lady Weatherby's, but the last thing I needed was for the head of the coven to think that I was mocking her on my wedding day. She'd probably hex me with a giant zit on the end of my nose and blame Agnes.

I stepped out of the dressing room and heard a collective gasp.

"Emma, there's no question. This one is made for you," Lucy said.

"Daniel is going to die," Sophie said dreamily.

"I certainly hope not," I said. "I want us to live a long and happy life together."

I looked at the admiring faces and suddenly felt Gareth's absence. As much as I loved the dress, I wanted his stamp of approval. He'd been getting better with manifesting in random places. I wondered whether he could manage the boutique.

"What do you think of this one?" Begonia asked, twirling around in a cornflower-blue tea-length dress.

"It matches your eyes perfectly," Sophie said. She wore a tangerine dress with a wrap-style bodice.

Lucy cast an appreciative glance at Sophie's choice. "That color really pops," she said.

Millie stepped out of the dressing room in a yellow strapless dress. She fidgeted with the top of her dress. "I think strapless might not be the best option."

"Agreed," Laurel said. "I'd rather be comfortable."

I laughed. "I've said it before, Laurel, but you truly are wise beyond your years."

Laurel's red dress was simple in the front with a huge bow on the back. "They're all so nice. How will you decide?"

My gaze swept across the choices. "Majority rules, I guess."

"Don't even consider mine," Millie said. "I'm taking it off now."

"I will speak to Leanne about the strapless one," Ricardo

said. "See if she can build in magic to make it more comfortable."

My ears perked up at the name. "Leanne?"

Ricardo nodded. "Yes, yes. My excellent pixie seamstress."

"Is she here now?" I asked.

Lucy elbowed me gently. "Emma, you're wearing a wedding dress. You can't possibly go and question someone now."

"I'll be right back." I hiked up my wedding dress and headed to the private rooms at the back of the shop.

A pixie with curly blonde hair fluttered in front of a sequined black dress, scrutinizing the cut. She reminded me of an old-fashioned doll, except for her visibly pregnant belly.

"You must be Leanne," I said. "Ricardo speaks very highly of you."

Leanne flashed a friendly smile. "Judging from your dress, you must be Emma. Ricardo was so happy when he found out you were engaged. You should've seen the way he danced around the shop."

I laughed. "I can only imagine. It looks like congratulations are in order to you, too."

Pink colored her cheeks. "Thank you. My husband and I have been trying for a while now, so this is a real blessing."

"Your husband is…?"

"Richard," she replied. "He works at the Spellbound Bank. He's the night manager there. It's actually where we met."

"Well, congratulations to both of you," I said. "If all goes well for you, you may not be doing the final tweaks on my wedding gown."

Her hands rested on her slightly swollen belly. "I promised Ricardo I would work as long as possible. I love my job." She glanced down at her future progeny. "But I will love my baby more. No question."

"Have you always wanted a family?" I asked.

Leanne nodded enthusiastically. "From the time I was a little girl, I pictured myself as a mother. Every game I played became a version of motherhood. In the woods behind my house, I used to tuck pinecones into little stick cribs." She smiled at the memory. "My mother says I was always destined for motherhood."

"I understand you used to be in a relationship with Seamus," I said. "I'm sorry for your loss."

Her expression clouded over. "Yes, I'm still trying to wrap my head around that one. I don't know why anyone would want to hurt him. Hemlock, was it?"

As usual, word spread rapidly in Spellbound. "That's what the report says."

Her sigh was full of regret. "Seamus was a wonderful pixie."

"But not wonderful enough to marry him," I remarked.

She shot me a curious look. "I would have married him in a heartbeat. He was the one with cold feet. I couldn't get him to commit to anything—a job, his favorite color, marriage… He knew how desperately I wanted children. Finally, I decided enough was enough."

"You broke things off?"

She couldn't meet my gaze. "I probably could have handled it better in retrospect. Like I said, I met Richard at the bank. He showed an interest in me right away and I could tell he was willing to settle down." She shrugged. "In the end, I decided he was a better option. I wasn't getting any younger and Seamus wasn't moving any faster."

"Were you angry with Seamus about that?" I asked. It must have been frustrating to invest years in the pixie without getting what she wanted out of the relationship.

She chewed her lip thoughtfully. "In the beginning, I was. I spent years with him, imagining what our family life would be like. I planned our future. I had no idea I would be dragging him into it." She heaved a sigh. "Eventually, I decided that I didn't want to drag anyone through life with me. I wanted him to come skipping and dancing because he was so happy to be with me. That wasn't going to be Seamus, no matter how desperately I wanted it to be."

"Why do you think he had a problem with commitment?" I asked.

She focused on the sequins, probably in an effort to keep her emotions in check. "He was always slow to make decisions. To commit to an opinion. He worried about making the wrong choice, so he never made any. But that's kind of like making a choice, isn't it?"

An idea occurred to me. "Maxwell said that you and Seamus spoke at the casino not long before he died. Did you tell him then that you were having a baby?"

Her hazel eyes squinted. "As a matter of fact, I did."

"What about Richard?" I asked. "How did he feel about your relationship with Seamus? Did he mind you sharing personal news with him at the casino?"

Leanne paused. "We argued about it later that night," she admitted. "Richard thinks I coddled him. He said that Seamus had his chance with me and blew it, so I should stop caring about his feelings." Leanne patted her belly. "Richard's going to make a great father. If I'm certain about one thing, it's that."

I studied her closely. "Do you love him? Richard, I mean."

"Of course I do," she replied hotly. "What kind of question is that?"

"Do you love him the way you loved Seamus?" I could tell the truth just by talking to her. I only wondered whether she recognized it herself.

"I love them for different reasons," she said. "They are two very different men. Or were. Seamus may have been indecisive and incommunicative, but he was easy to love."

"And Richard?" I prompted.

Her jaw tensed. "Richard is stable and certain. He'll take good care of us. That's the most important thing."

I had to admit, there were worse reasons to choose a partner. "You said Richard is the night manager at the bank?"

"That's right. He goes in at four o'clock."

"That might be a tough schedule for your family once the baby comes," I said.

Her expression brightened. "He's already put in to change shifts when the baby comes. He thinks ahead like that. That's what I mean about two different men. Seamus struggled to commit to a career. Richard has a five-year plan."

I opted not to point out that a five-year plan wouldn't have done poor Seamus much good under the circumstances.

"Best of luck with the baby," I said.

"Best of luck with your wedding," she replied. "Maybe the next time we meet up, you'll be in here for maternity clothes."

Now it was my turn to blush. "Baby steps, Leanne...I mean, slow and steady."

CHAPTER 7

Are you sure you want to accompany me here? I asked. *Don't forget she has that cat that doesn't like owls.*

Bella, Sedgwick reminded me. *I'm not afraid of anyone's familiar. I have one huge advantage over her.*

What's that? Your sassy attitude?

No, oh ye of little brains. Wings.

Who are you calling a birdbrain, you birdbrain? I shot back.

Very mature, Sedgwick said.

Stay up high while we're here and Bella will have no chance of catching you, I instructed him.

That's the plan. Besides, last time I was here I found a nest of voles in the woods behind her house. That's my first stop.

I should've known you didn't come just to support me, I said.

I'll support you from the woods while I indulge my inner predator.

Have fun, I called with a wave. I parked Sigmund in the driveway and went straight out to the backyard. There was no need to go to the front door. I knew from previous experience that Janis Goodfellow spent the majority of her time tending to her garden. As an herbologist in the coven, she was dedicated to all species of plants and herbs, and, therefore, the perfect witch to ask about hemlock.

Bella found me first. The large cat trotted toward me, sniffing the air. I had no doubt she smelled Sedgwick.

"Hello there, Bella," I said. "Is your witch at home?"

"As a matter of fact, she is," a voice said. Janis appeared around the corner of the house. As I expected, she wore gardening gloves and kneepads. Her wide-brimmed hat was clutched in her hand.

"Good to see you, Janis," I said. "How have you been?"

She smiled. "Not as good as you, sorceress. I understand there are nuptials on the horizon with that angel of yours."

"There are," I replied. "I know I shouldn't be surprised that word gets around."

She wiped the sweat from her brow. "The only thing anyone can talk about more is the coven working to break the curse. That part is hush-hush, though, so your wedding is the talk of the rest of the town."

"Is anyone taking bets on whether it happens?"

Janis chuckled. "Some folks are always looking for an excuse to gamble. You know that." She paused. "But you should know the odds are in your favor."

"Phew. I'd be more offended if they were betting against us." I watched as Bella went and wrapped her furry body around Janis's legs.

Janis glanced down at the large cat. "I guess you don't have this kind of relationship with your familiar. Kinda difficult to be affectionate with an owl."

"Sedgwick is affectionate in his own way," I said. Okay, so we would never snuggle at night or he'd never tickle my skin with his soft fur, but I appreciated our special connection all the same.

Janis reached down to stroke Bella's back. "So I imagine

you're not here to feel sorry for yourself. What do you need? Some plant for the spell that breaks the curse?"

"Oh, I'm not working on that," I said. "That's a select group that doesn't include me."

Janis frowned. "That's foolish. You're the lone sorceress here. You should be part of those meetings."

"I'm not really sure what good I would be. I don't really understand my powers very well. Laurel is better at figuring things out. I just sort of bumble along."

Janis removed her gardening gloves and tossed them onto the ground. "If anybody thinks that you don't have a role to play in breaking the curse, they are bigger idiots than I thought."

"Maybe you should share your feelings with Lady Weatherby," I said. I knew perfectly well that she wouldn't. Nobody challenged Lady Weatherby.

"You know what? I just might. She's been a good leader, but I haven't agreed with many of her decisions in recent times. And I've never been much of a shrinking violet. I should speak up."

She began to walk around the back of the house toward her garden and I followed. "Do you think you would leave Spellbound if we break the curse?" It seemed to me that Janis had everything she could ever want right here. I couldn't envision her leaving her wonderful garden. Not after she'd spent her whole life tending to it.

"I certainly wouldn't move," she said. "But I would love to travel. There are places I long to see. The gardens of Versailles are on my cauldron list."

"I hear it's beautiful there," I said. I'd never been to France. My grandparents hadn't been keen on travel. "I need to talk to you about hemlock."

Her brow lifted. "Hemlock?"

I nodded. "The autopsy report came back on Seamus, the pixie who died recently. It showed hemlock in his system."

Janis whistled. "Not a fun way to go."

"Not at all," I replied. "I'd like to know more about it and I figure you're the best one to ask."

"Nobody ever called you stupid." Janis studied me. "Listen, Emma. I'm going to trust you with something. Are you ready for it?"

Her tone made me uneasy. "Do I want to know?" Some secrets were best left alone. Whatever she had up her sleeve, I wasn't sure I wanted the burden of this information.

Janis walked along the stone pathway to an empty patch of grass at the back of the garden. Sedgwick circled overhead, observing us.

Why are you staring at an empty part of the garden? he queried.

I don't know yet. Be quiet and I'll find out.

Janis produced her wand from her waistband and said, "Smaller than an elephant, bigger than a mouse/remove the barrier and reveal my greenhouse."

The air in front of us shimmered and I recognized the outline of a greenhouse. At first it reminded me of a hologram, until finally it stood before us, completely solid and real.

I shot her a quizzical look. "Why a secret greenhouse?"

"Step inside and you'll see," she said.

Janis opened the door to the greenhouse and I followed her inside. The room was about the size of my dining room and it was filled with plants I didn't recognize.

Janis stopped in front of a row of plants that stretched all the way to the ceiling. "Do you remember how I petitioned the council to keep poisonous plants?"

"Yes, and they denied your request."

"Let's just say Janis Goodfellow doesn't take no for an answer."

I surveyed the interior of the greenhouse. "These are all poisonous plants?"

"That's right." She gestured behind her. "These are mandrakes. I've got hemlock, nightshade, henbane, wolfsbane. Name one and I probably have it here."

"So you've created a secret greenhouse to circumvent the council's order?"

"The study of these plants is essential," Janis said. "I have a concealment spell on the greenhouse, so no one even knows it exists. I can't create a health and safety issue or attract criminals if no one knows about it. But I get to study my plants without interference from the council."

"Does Lady Weatherby know?" I asked.

Janis arched an eyebrow. "What do you think? She's the head of the coven. First and foremost, she's a rule follower. You and I both know that rules need to be flexible."

"What makes you think I agree with you?" I asked.

She barked a short laugh. "Emma Hart, do you think I haven't been paying attention? You want to revise the sentencing guidelines. You defend criminals with the compassion of their mothers. If anyone wants rules to be fluid here, it's you."

"In the human world, we call that a bleeding heart liberal," I said. "Although it's often used as an insult."

"Well, I won't insult you with it. And I'm trusting you with my secret."

"Why?" In my mind, every additional paranormal who knew was a liability.

"You want to learn about hemlock," Janis said. "I can do better than tell you. I can show you." She went over to another table and pointed. "I bet you don't even realize there are two types of hemlock. Well, here they are. Look and learn."

"As a matter of fact, I didn't know." I scrutinized the tall plants on the table. "One looks like a fern and one looks like Queen Ann's lace. What's the difference?"

"The one that looks like Queen Ann's lace is actually water hemlock. It can reach about eight feet high in the wild. See there, it has compound leaves with small white flowers. The roots are hollow but contain the highest concentration of toxins."

"Wow," I said. "And I guess it's mostly found near bodies of water."

"Not necessarily, although it does like moist habitats," Janis replied. "The fern-like one is called poison or deadly hemlock. It can grow higher than eight feet and has purple spots on the flowers. Like water hemlock, the roots are most dangerous and are often mistaken for wild parsnip."

"The leaves remind me of parsley," I said. I reached out to touch them, but Janis slapped my hand away.

"Touching is a bad idea unless you're wearing gloves," Janis said.

"This has all been fascinating," I said. "I do worry about your greenhouse, though. What if your concealment spell breaks? Then you have an entire poisonous garden that becomes vulnerable to less-than-scrupulous paranormals."

"They still have to know about its existence," she said. "Not many folks come out here unless they're coming to see me. Even then, they would only see a normal-looking greenhouse."

"So if I'm looking for a supply of hemlock, who are the usual suspects?"

Janis pressed her lips together. "You didn't hear it from me, but I've heard that Frank has been known to trade in illegal plants on occasion. You might want to start with him."

"The gnome that runs the Enchanted Garden?" I queried.

She touched her finger to her nose. "That's him. Nice fella. I don't think he would knowingly provide it to someone who wanted to commit murder, but still worth a conversation."

"What other reason would there be to acquire hemlock?" I asked. As far as I knew, it wasn't a remedy for any maladies.

"For academic reasons like mine," Janis said. She left the greenhouse with Bella trailing behind her. I quickly hurried to catch up, unsure what would happen if the concealment spell went into effect while I was still inside.

"I highly doubt Frank is selling hemlock to an underground team of academics," I said. I watched as she produced her wand again and reset the spell. The greenhouse disappeared from view.

"Rest assured, mine will never find its way into idle hands," Janis said. "And I meant what I said about you being part of the team that breaks the curse. I may not be as powerful a witch as Lady Weatherby, but I have a sixth sense about these things. Every time you're near me, all I can think of is freedom."

I didn't know what to say to that. It felt like a lot of pressure on one sorceress's shoulders. "I'll talk to Laurel and see what kind of progress they're making. If it seems like there's some way I can be useful, I'll say so."

Janis patted my shoulder. "If there's one thing you do well, Emma, it's advocate. I guess that's the lawyer in you, getting things done."

I met her admiring gaze. "You get things done, too, Janis. And I'm pretty sure that's the woman in both of us."

Darkness enveloped me as I stood in the middle of the forest alone. The full moon shone down on me like a giant spotlight. I glanced down at my clothes. Why was I in a white nightgown? I didn't even own a white nightgown. More importantly, was it see-through in the moonlight because I also seemed to be wearing oversized granny underpants?

It's quite the virginal look, Sedgwick said, circling the treetops.

Is this a dream? I asked.

If it was, don't you think you'd make yourself look better? At least carry a comb in your pocket for hair emergencies.

Wow. Dream Sedgwick was as cantankerous as Reality Sedgwick.

Since when do you criticize my hair? I asked. *That's Gareth's job.*

He's not here, the owl replied. *Someone has to take responsibility.*

Here. Where was here? I surveyed the area carefully, uncertain which part of the forest I was in. Was this where I encountered the sacred unicorn? No, there was no body of water nearby. Only trees.

"I don't see the way out," I called. The trees were dense and there was no obvious path. Was I in the Pines, the section of town where a lot of the shifters lived?

There is no way out, Sedgwick said from above.

"Of course there is," I replied. "I just need to find it." I tripped over a log and nearly fell on my face. If I cracked my skull in a dream, would I wake up with a headache? Ugh, I hoped not. I had too much to do during daylight hours to deal with a headache.

Use your broom, Sedgwick said.

My hands flew testily to my hips. "Do I look like I have my broom?"

Hard to tell with all those branches down there, Sedgwick replied.

"If this is a dream, maybe you can help me wake up," I

said. "Drop something on my head. Nothing too heavy, though." Still wanted to avoid a headache.

Sedgwick scanned the area. *What am I supposed to drop? It's not like there are any coconut trees.*

Okay, if waking up wasn't an option, then I needed to find another way. I studied the trees. They were too close together for me to walk between them. I was basically in a woodland cage.

"I need a spell that moves a couple of these trees," I said. "Or maybe if I turn them into rubber, they'll bend."

Flaunt it if you've got it, Sedgwick said.

I focused my will and stretched out my arms like I was preparing to give the earth a bear hug. Power surged through me and streamed from my fingertips with such intensity that my skin burned. The air around me thickened until the pressure became too much and the ground shook. I worried that the earth was about to swallow me whole. I was thrown to the ground by something akin to a sonic boom. My tailbone hit the dirt and I cried out in pain.

Your Highness? Sedgwick called, concerned.

When I finally recovered and stood to get my bearings, I realized that every tree around me had been ripped from its roots and tossed on the forest floor like kindling. I could see for miles around me.

"Stars and stones," I whispered, turning slowly to get a view from every angle. The entire forest was decimated. I'd detonated a magical bomb.

What a mess, Sedgwick said. *Remind me never to take you anywhere.*

I glanced upward, relieved that my familiar was unharmed. "Sedgwick, what on earth happened?"

You did, he replied.

CHAPTER 8

THE ENCHANTED GARDEN was the garden center owned by Frank, the gnome that allegedly dabbled in illegal substances. He was married to Myra, the church administrator. You only needed to look at him to know that he and Myra were made for each other. With their black shoes, chubby faces, and pointy little hats, they looked like bookends. Frank's cheeks were perpetually rosy, giving the impression that he either suffered from rosacea or carried a hip flask.

"Hey, Frank," I said, weaving between the rows of plants, flowers, and trees. The sudden burst of smells and scents threatened to overwhelm me.

The gnome hurried forward to shake my hand. "Emma Hart, so good to see you. What brings you in here? Something new for your garden? I pass by many a time and remark to Myra what an improvement there's been since you moved in. Not so much of the gloom and doom that appealed to Gareth."

"Tell the conehead that not everyone needs a riot of color to feel cheerful," Gareth said, taking me by surprise.

I whipped around at the sound of his voice. "What are you doing here?"

Gareth spread his arms wide. "What do you think? I've been practicing. Apparently, the Enchanted Garden is one of the places I can access quite easily, not that I'm particularly interested in hanging around here."

Frank looked from me to the blank space, his face ashen. "Is Gareth here?"

I folded my arms. "It seems I have a shadow."

"You're the one who's been pestering me to leave the house," Gareth said. "Now you're going to complain when I actually manage it? You're as difficult as my Aunt Caitriona."

"She can't be that difficult," I countered. "I've never once heard you complain about her. Goodness knows I've heard a thousand stories of your tough Scottish upbringing by now."

"I heard the great news about your wedding," Frank said. "Daniel is a lucky angel as far as I'm concerned."

My heart skipped a beat the way it always did when Daniel's name was mentioned. "I don't know about that," I said. "I still pinch myself every morning when I wake up."

Gareth nodded beside me. "She really does. I've seen her. Quite pathetic, to be honest."

I glared at him. "First of all, Frank can't hear you. Second of all, why are you watching me wake up? That's creepy."

Gareth shrugged. "I get bored. You overestimate what a vampire ghost has to do in a town like Spellbound."

"So back to business," Frank said. "If you're not looking for garden improvements, it must be something for your wedding."

I took an unexpected interest in all of the plants and flowers around me. I'd assumed we would get our arrangements from Petals like everyone else, but standing in the garden center, an idea began to form.

"Now that you mention it, you have amazing stock here,"

I said. "I'd love to be able to incorporate some of your inventory."

The little gnome rubbed his hands together eagerly. "I've always wanted to work on a wedding. Myra gets to participate in weddings all the time over at the church, but nobody ever thinks of the garden center."

"I'll have to bring Daniel back with me one day to discuss ideas," I said, "but now I have this amazing vision for the lake."

Frank's eyes rounded. "You want to have your wedding at Swan Lake?"

"What can I say?" Gareth said. "She's a glutton for punishment."

I attempted to elbow Gareth in the ribs, but my arm only met with air.

"We're reclaiming the location as ours," I said. "We share a special memory of that place, and we're not going to let one bad moment ruin it."

Frank grinned and I noticed a sparkle in his eyes. "I'm already seeing it. Floating flowers across the shimmering lake, all the way to the border."

"We can choose flowers that complement the bridesmaid dresses," I said excitedly. "And have an arched trellis covered in ivy where Daniel and I recite our vows."

Even Gareth joined in the vision. "Dust his wings with silver glitter for maximum impact."

"It's a wedding, not a disco," I said. "Frank, I have to tell you, you're as good as any muse." And I thought meeting with Haley was inspiring. Standing in the Enchanted Garden, the possibilities seemed endless. I became so entranced, I nearly forgot the reason I was here. Nearly, but not quite.

"Frank, as much as I'd love to talk more about the

wedding, there's a more important matter that I need to address."

Frank tipped back his hat. "More important than your wedding? Yes, of course. Whatever you need."

"I'm not here to rat you out, but I have it on good authority that you may, on occasion, trade in illegal substances."

Concern flashed in his beady eyes. I could tell he was debating whether to come clean or feign innocence. "I'm not sure exactly what you've been told, but I may have helped acquire certain difficult-to-obtain substances from time to time if a paranormal is in dire need. But I never do it for nefarious purposes."

Beside me, Gareth made an impressed noise. "Nefarious, now there's a big word for a small gnome."

I ignored him. "I promise I'm not here to get you in trouble, Frank, although I think you need to be more careful. I'm trying to track down where Seamus's murderer may have acquired hemlock."

Frank balked. "Seamus died from hemlock poisoning?"

I nodded. "That's what the autopsy report shows. To my knowledge, hemlock is pretty easy to identify. It's not likely to be confused with any other poison."

"Not once it's ingested, no," Frank said. He bowed his head. "Poor Seamus. I knew the pixie a bit. He seemed like a decent fella. That's a fairly unpleasant way to go."

"Yes, his neighbor was traumatized. He was the one who found him."

Frank rubbed his auburn beard. "On the one hand, I wish I could help you. On the other hand, I'm happy to report I haven't supplied anyone with hemlock. Ever."

"Have you heard of anyone asking about hemlock?" A shot in the dark.

Frank took a moment to consider the question, but eventually shook his head. "It's the kind of thing I pay attention to as well. I'd certainly remember if someone was making inquiries about a lethal substance like that."

So he was as plugged in to town gossip as his nosy wife. That didn't surprise me.

"So are we done here?" Gareth asked.

I gave him a sharp look. "What? Now you have better things to do?"

Gareth offered a sheepish smile. "Now that I know I can come here, I want to give Ready-to-Were a try. That way I can be there for dress fittings. I'm already worried about decisions that have been made without me."

I shook my head. "Has anyone ever told you that you have control issues?"

"That's the cauldron calling the kettle black," Gareth said.

"Fine, but the dressing rooms are off limits."

"No worries there," Gareth said. "The only bum I want to see in the mirror is my own."

"There's the blushing bride-to-be," Myra said, bustling down the church aisle toward me. The gnome was uncharacteristically happy to see me. I had no doubt it was so that she could inspect the ring on my finger and pass along her first-hand knowledge. Myra was one of the premier gossips in town. She treated residents who used the confessional like gossip column informants.

"Good evening, Myra," I said. "I take it your husband told you about the engagement."

The gnome nodded her chubby head. "I haven't seen Frank this excited since Amanda made a gnome in his image. You have no idea how long he's been wanting to participate in a wedding. I've been telling him for years that he should open up to compete with Petals. There's no reason why that place should get every wedding in town. A little healthy competition is good for everyone."

"I think Frank's inventory will lend itself better to our vision for the wedding," I said. "I have nothing against Petals." The flower shop was perfect for basic needs, but now that I had a glimpse of what this wedding could be, I knew that Frank's Enchanted Garden was the right decision.

"I will say I was disappointed that Daniel decided not to hold the ceremony here," Myra said. "After all, he *is* an angel." She gestured to the stained glass windows and pews surrounding us. "This should be his house of worship."

Not since they booted him, I wanted to say. Instead, I said, "It's a shame the church isn't bigger. We'd like to include as many residents as possible."

Myra seemed to view the church through my eyes. "Yes, I guess our capacity is limited. Such a beautiful setting, though. It's a shame to not take advantage of it."

It really was. There was an old church not far from Lemon Grove that I used to admire from the outside as I drove past. It had enormous arched windows and dramatic spires. I felt an unexpected pang of longing for the familiar.

"We're fortunate to have a place like this in town," I said. Even though I only came here for harp therapy, I knew it served as a refuge for many others.

Myra patted the top edge of the pew. "It's my home away from home."

The sound of harps from the basement signaled that I was officially late for harp therapy class.

"I've got to run, but it was nice to see you, Myra," I said politely.

"Of course, of course," Myra said. "You'd better get down there. You don't want to get stuck next to that horrid Phoebe Minor."

I didn't have the heart to tell her that I actually enjoyed

the older harpy's company. As long as her sharp tongue wasn't directed at me, Phoebe was one of the most entertaining residents in Spellbound.

I headed downstairs and was disappointed to see that the plates of brownies and other treats were already gone. One of the perks of harp therapy class was the delicious snacks at the start. Paisley, the witch from Mix-n-Match and the object of Britta's affections, waved me over. She motioned to the empty seat beside her and I crept between the chairs to get there, not wanting to disturb anyone's rhythm.

"Congratulations," Paisley whispered.

"Thank you," I said, sliding into the seat. "I feel like everyone in town has congratulated me this week."

"That's what happens when the most famous sorceress in town becomes engaged to the only fallen angel in town," she replied. "One of you alone would be a big deal. The two of you joining together...It's unprecedented."

I suddenly felt like a celebrity power couple, like Brad Pitt and Angelina Jolie, back when they were actually still together. There was a reason those marriages didn't stand the test of time and I had a feeling public scrutiny was a big part of it. Thankfully, Spellbound was only a microcosm, far too small to interfere with the success of our marriage.

"Here's Emma," Phoebe said loudly. "Probably late for some wedding-related reason. I bet you're still bride-ing high, aren't you?"

"She is a bride-or-die chick," Sheena added.

Melvin tittered. "She's fit to be bride."

"Okay, okay," I said. "You're all hilarious with your bridal puns. While we're on the subject of my wedding, I have a very important question for all of you."

"What's that?" Phoebe asked. "You need pointers for your wedding night? I'm sure I can offer you some tips. Daniel can thank me later." She gave me a wink.

I cringed at the thought of getting sex advice from the older harpy. "Thank you, but no. Daniel and I have been discussing our musical options for the wedding, and we've decided that it would be nice to have harp music during the ceremony. I would love it if any or all of you would be willing to play for us."

A hush fell over the room. Finally, Phoebe spoke.

"Are you ill?" she asked. She glanced helplessly around the church basement. "Is there any disease brought on by an engagement?"

"No, of course not. I feel fine," I said.

Phoebe pinned a cautious gaze on me. "You're not dying, are you? Because that would put a serious damper on your wedding."

I laughed nervously. "Not to my knowledge. Why would you ask that?"

"Because we're terrible harpists," Sheena blurted. "We come here to eat sweets and gossip. Nobody is any good at the harp. You must be out of your mind."

"Speak for yourself," Melvin interjected.

"You should get Look Mom, No Wings," Britta said. "That band is awesome."

"They definitely are, Britta. I've seen them play at Moon-shine and they are awesome, but I'm not talking about the reception. I'm talking about the ceremony at Swan Lake."

"You'd be better off releasing a bunch of doves and then strangling them," Phoebe said. "The sound would be far more pleasant."

I smiled. "Phoebe, you vastly underestimate the talent of everyone here. I come because the music is relaxing. Okay, we get the occasional squeak or unwanted sound, but I think you'd all bring something special to our wedding. Trust me, Daniel never would have agreed to it if he thought you were rubbish."

"Rubbish?" Phoebe echoed. "You've clearly been spending too much time with that grumpy Scottish vampire of yours."

"Kinda hard to avoid, given that he lives with me," I said.

"How's that going to work once you're married?" Britta asked. "Threesomes are cool and all, but I'm surprised Daniel would be down with that."

Paisley shot the Valkyrie a curious look. "Threesomes are cool, are they?"

"That's what I've heard," Britta said quickly. "From, you know, other paranormals who might have engaged in that sort of behavior."

My cheeks grew flushed. "I think it's important to remember that Gareth is a ghost."

"Yes, but I've heard he's getting better at manifesting," Paisley said. "He's able to solidify his form, right?"

"On occasion," I said, unsurprised by the rumors. "He still hasn't fully mastered the skill. He's been working with Lyra Grey. He's made great progress, but he still has a way to go." In truth, I secretly hoped he'd be as solid as possible for the wedding. He'd already started practicing manifesting at Swan Lake so that he was sure he could attend. As long as we could see each other, we'd be content with that. I knew he was looking forward to the reception so he could dance with his vampire friends. Daniel and I needed to decide on a reception venue, mainly so that Gareth could practice showing up there.

"Which songs would you like us to play at the wedding, Emma?" Melvin asked. "I think we should start preparing now. We don't have very long to perfect it."

"I'm not looking for perfection," I said. "I'm just happy you all want to be there and participate in our special day."

Phoebe groaned. "That sounds so lame. It's your wedding day. Do you know how lucky you are to have one of those? The harpies in my house would kill for the chance to have a perfect wedding. We're going to practice until our fingers bleed."

The horrified looks on the other faces suggested otherwise.

"No one's hands will be bleeding because of me," I insisted. "I mean it, Phoebe. I'm happy to have you all there. The more love that surrounds us, the more special it will be."

Phoebe blew a raspberry. "If you say so."

I flashed her a charming smile. "I say so."

CHAPTER 9

"MEMBERS OF THE COVEN, Miss Hart has kindly agreed to join us for this meeting," Lady Weatherby said. Her tone was so neutral, I couldn't decide whether she was annoyed or pleased that Janis Goodfellow had demanded my involvement. "The hope is that her role as a sorceress might offer us guidance in breaking the curse."

"It's about time," Meg said. "I've been suggesting your presence for weeks."

I heard faint noises of approval, although Lady Weatherby appeared miffed by the comment. "And so your wish has been granted, Margaret. Had I believed Miss Hart would be of use to us, I certainly would have agreed to her inclusion sooner. The reality is, though, that she is only now beginning to scratch the surface of her abilities. I am not entirely convinced she will have any helpful insight at this juncture."

So, basically, the head of the coven just called me useless. Gee, thanks for the vote of confidence.

"Thank you for including me," I said. "I'll do my best to help." As I claimed the empty seat beside Laurel, I noticed Beatrice at the far end of the table. She didn't seem at all pleased to see me. She probably still resented me for attracting the attention of Markos.

Spread across the wooden table in front of me were various parchments with unfamiliar writing. Some of it I recognized from the secret lair when Laurel discovered the hidden information. There had been previous efforts to find a way to break the curse, so we were building on work that had already been done.

"Where's the unicorn horn?" I asked.

"Safe in the coven vault and warded to the hilt," Ginger replied. "We decided to keep it there until we need it. There's no point in risking its safety."

"Do you think it would be in any danger?" I asked. "I would think most paranormals, if not all, want to see an end to the curse."

"The horn of a sacred unicorn carries incredible power," Professor Holmes explained. "The more unscrupulous among us might try to use such an item for personal gain."

I studied the parchment. "So how far have we gotten with deciphering?"

"Laurel's been a welcome addition," Meg said. "She's managed to translate an entire paragraph that had us all stumped."

Out of the corner of my eye, I caught Laurel's proud smile. I had no doubt I was looking at the future head of the coven. Laurel was smart, capable, and respected at a very young age, not unlike the lauded Arabella St. Simon. It wouldn't have surprised me at all to learn they were related.

"Laurel, why don't you tell Emma about your findings?" Ginger said.

"These symbols represent chains or bonds," Laurel said, tapping on the parchment.

I looked at the circular symbols and immediately thought

of Daniel's halo. He was never far from my thoughts, even when I needed to focus on other matters.

"They want us to break the chains?" I queried. "I guess that makes sense."

"That was the assumption we'd been working under," Professor Holmes said.

I shot a quizzical look at Laurel. "We shouldn't break the chains?" I was confused.

"I don't think the symbols here represent the curse," Laurel said. "Obviously, we should break the curse. I think the chains refer to something else."

I squinted at the parchment. "That looks like a harp."

Laurel's eyes shone brightly. "I think so, too."

"We need to play harp music to break the curse?" Because that could be easily arranged.

"No," Laurel said. "It's not literal. The harp is an ancient symbol that represents a ladder or a bridge."

I peered at the image. "To where? The human world?"

"I think so," Laurel said. "Or maybe other paranormal towns. Either way, it suggests a way out of Spellbound."

"An exit sign would be even better," I said. No one laughed. The coven was a tough crowd.

"The strings are like the rungs of a ladder," Laurel explained, pointing to the harp symbol. "In some ancient cultures, they symbolized a pathway to paradise."

"I'd hardly call the human world paradise," I joked.

"For the Celts, the harp symbolized a bridge of love," Professor Holmes said. "The connection between heaven and earth."

Something awful occurred to me. "Does that suggest the only way out is death?"

"We assume not," Lady Weatherby said. "Although with references to paradise and heaven, it's not out of the realm of possibility."

I thought of the different wards we discussed in class recently. "Could it also mean if we break the curse, we all die?" I asked. "Maybe the curse is booby-trapped. If we trip the alarm, the whole thing blows."

Lady Weatherby's perfectly sculpted cheek twitched. "We cannot know unless we try. Otherwise, we resign ourselves to this fate."

"Further research is needed, of course," Professor Holmes said. "There are more books with potential information than we have time to read."

"Maybe the net you're casting is too wide," I suggested. "When I used to practice law, if we had a client with limited resources, we had to be very targeted in our searches because we couldn't spend too much money. A wide net would have meant a much bigger bill and an unhappy client."

"And we have limited resources," Professor Holmes murmured.

"Is there a reason we need to keep this so quiet?" I asked. "I know you don't want to get everyone's hopes up, but if you need more help, I bet paranormals would line up to offer assistance."

Lady Weatherby shook her head. "We can't have too many witches near the cauldron. It spoils the stew."

"We can't have the parchments accessible to everyone," Meg said. "They're too valuable."

"We've made copies before," I countered. "Why not copies to distribute to the masses? Let others swarm the town library and have the witches and warlocks use the coven library."

Lady Weatherby stared out the window, contemplating my suggestion. "I shall take it under advisement."

"I don't mean to be difficult…" I began.

Lady Weatherby turned to face me. "And yet here you are."

"What's your objection to more help?" I asked. "Why are you so afraid to give residents information? There are a lot of intelligent paranormals out there who want to break this curse as much as you do. Even your mother would have insight into this."

"If my mother had insight into this," Lady Weatherby said in a clipped tone, "then she would have broken the curse when the coven was under her control."

Right. I decided not to push the issue any further. Not today. I'd only just been invited to the meetings and I'd already annoyed the leader. Well done, me.

"Just so we're clear, the information stays within the coven for now," Lady Weatherby said. "I've been giving regular updates to the council, of course, but let that be the extent of it."

I nodded mutely. If I expected to be invited back, I had to accept the terms. Unfortunately, that meant no Grey sisters or Raisa. Lady Weatherby had her reasons for playing this close to the vest and I had to respect them, whether I agreed or not. Of course, nothing she said would prevent me from sharing Laurel's information with Agnes. After all, the elderly witch was technically still a member of the coven.

I smiled to myself as the meeting was adjourned. In the care home, Agnes' hands were nothing but idle. It was time to put them to work.

After an afternoon in the office trying to convince Althea that I didn't need garden gnomes as a wedding present, I decided to pay a visit to Leanne's husband, Richard. The Spellbound Bank was located on the side of town near the library. Instead of waiting in the teller line, I went to the seated area where the manager's desk was located. I grabbed a lollipop from the counter and popped it into my mouth while I waited for the man I identified as Richard. He was mid-conversation with another customer. With a buzz cut and a neatly pressed dress shirt, he looked as dry and reliable as I expected. While I'd initially considered telling Astrid what I was up to, I had a few financial questions to ask anyway, so I opted to speak to him solo. Two birds, one bank visit.

Richard beckoned me over once the other customer had vacated the seat.

"Good afternoon, miss," he greeted me. "How can I help you today?" His smile was perfunctory, like the rest of him.

I took the lollipop out of my mouth to speak. "I have a few questions that I hope you can answer. First, I'd like to know what kind of lollipop this is and why it tastes like starmark juice."

Richard looked at me like I was an alien who'd just announced my intention to lord over his people. "You've never had a Wishpop?"

I glanced at the lollipop in my hand. "I guess not. What is it?"

"The lollipop tastes however you want it to taste," he explained. "It's a blank slate waiting for your input."

"How have I never heard of these?" I licked it again. Yep, starmark juice.

"We always keep them on the counters here," Richard said, without cracking a smile. "You can buy them in bulk at the Wish Market."

"Good to know." Great. A new food obsession. Just what I needed before my wedding. "Now that the mystery of the lollipop is solved, I'd like information about setting up a trust fund at the bank."

He clasped his hands together on the desk. "We can certainly help with that. I'll need some basic information like your name, address, the recipient's name..."

"About that…" Was I really going to ask? I gulped. Apparently, I was. "What if the recipient is a cat?"

He looked unperturbed. "You mean a familiar?"

"No, I mean a domestic cat." A hellbeast, more accurately, but Richard didn't need to know the specifics.

"And you want this trust in place so that there are funds to care for the cat in the event of your death?" he asked.

"Yes," I said. The possibility had been on my mind ever since the trials to obtain the unicorn horn. If something had happened to me then, I realized that Magpie would've been left adrift. I couldn't risk that happening. Even if Gareth improved his interaction with the physical world tenfold, he'd still be a ghost. Magpie needed someone…alive. Or at least not dead undead.

"How old is the cat?" he asked.

"No idea," I replied. It wouldn't surprise me to learn that Magpie used to run amok with the dinosaurs. "I'm also thinking that if I decide to move in with my fiancé once we're married, I'd like to have money in a trust to pay for the upkeep of the house where the cat would continue to live. I wouldn't want to relocate Magpie." I didn't mention Gareth. It didn't seem necessary.

Incredibly, Richard acted like this was the most normal request in the world and that he could—and would—handle it. In that moment, I understood what Leanne saw in him. Maxwell was right; Richard's can-do attitude was probably in direct contrast to Seamus's.

"I'm not sure you need a trust for that," Richard said. "Maybe just a separate account dedicated to the cat's living expenses."

"You don't think it's a strange request?" I asked. I did, and I was the one asking.

"It's not strange at all," he said. "You'd be surprised by the types of requests we get here at the bank. I would also recommend speaking to a lawyer about a will that mentions the trust and leaves clear instructions for the house. Don't leave a mess for your heirs to clean up."

"Don't worry about that," I said. "I'm a lawyer, so I was planning to take care of that part myself."

Richard gave a curt nod. "Then you know all about it."

And now it was time for Questions for Richard, Part Deux. "I had the pleasure of meeting your wife recently at Ready-to-Were," I said. "Congratulations on your bundle of joy."

Richard offered a genuine smile this time. "Thank you so much. We couldn't be more thrilled."

"It's a shame that such a happy time has to coincide with Seamus's death. I know how much Leanne cared about him."

Richard sniffed. "That pixie wasn't good enough for her. Never was. That's not to say I'm not sorry about his death. It's always sad when someone goes before his time. Seamus still had his whole life ahead of him."

Well, that seemed like a perfectly sensible response. Not the reply of an angry, jealous killer.

"I understand you saw Seamus recently at the casino," I said, and watched closely for a reaction.

His expression hardened, a shift that emphasized his square jaw. "I saw him, but that's it. We didn't exchange words. I left that to Leanne. She's always had a soft spot for him, even after the breakup."

"Did that bother you at all? Her soft spot for him?"

"Of course it did," he said. "That being said, it's one of the qualities I love about Leanne—her soft heart. Balances out my coldness nicely."

"I know we only just met, but you don't strike me as a cold fish," I said. Polite and perfunctory, yes. Cold and calculating, no.

"That's kind of you to say," Richard said. "But I know my

shortcomings. I call them as I see them and I don't sugarcoat anything. I do express my feelings—I'll say that much—but they're not always as compassionate as Leanne's."

Richard had more in common with my therapist than he knew.

"Leanne mentioned that the two of you had an argument after the casino about Seamus," I said.

His thick eyebrows knitted together. "I didn't want to see her getting stuck in again. He was having some issues and I could see her wanting to help, but we have our own family to focus on now. Seamus is...was a grown pixie. He needed to handle his own business without Leanne's constant emotional support."

"Were you angry with Seamus?" I queried.

He gave a dismissive shake of his head. "It's hard to be angry at a guy like that. He was too nice. A sad sack, but nice. Too bad his older brother inherited the werelion's share of the good genes."

Wait, what? "His older brother?" I queried. Now that I thought about it, someone had mentioned a brother. For some reason, I'd assumed he was younger than Seamus, probably because the house was left to Seamus.

"Sean," Richard said. "He's a counselor over at the high school. From what Leanne has told me, he's the opposite of Seamus. Very pulled together."

"If Sean is older, why was Seamus the one who inherited the house?" I asked.

Richard's eyes lit up. "Oh, yes. I recall Leanne telling me about resentment between the brothers because of that. I don't know the details, though. You'd have to ask Sean."

Oh, I definitely would. "Thanks for your time, Richard. And congratulations on the baby. I wish you all the luck in the world. I know the two of you are going to make great parents."

"Thank you," he replied. "Let me know when you're ready to make a decision on the trust. Spellbound Bank is always here to help."

"Thanks, Richard. I will." On the way out, I plucked another Wishpop from the counter and focused on the taste of my grandmother's homemade lemonade. The flavor melted in my mouth. If there was one thing I'd learned in Spellbound, it was that even the smallest acts of magic could pack a powerful emotional punch.

CHAPTER 10

I STARED at the tower of books in front of me, my eyes burning from fatigue.

"I'm glad they decided to include you," Laurel said.

"I'm not sure 'they' decided, so much as Janis Goodfellow kicked up a fuss," I said.

We sat at a table in the library with more books than we could possibly get through in one sitting. Laurel wanted to research additional symbols and I'd volunteered to help. Although it was past her curfew, her mother said it was fine as long as she was with me and we stayed in the library. In other words, no Horned Owl, not that I would ever be irresponsible enough to have Laurel accompany me there. I may be flexible in my approach to rules, like Janis claimed, but not when it came to other paranormals' children.

Laurel thumbed her way through one book after another. At the rate she moved, she put speed-readers to shame. She was so focused on her own task that it took her a full twenty minutes to realize I was no longer looking through her chosen pile of books on ancient symbols.

"Why do you have a book on ghosts?" she queried.

Although I tried to keep the cover somewhat hidden, I should have known Laurel would be too perceptive.

"I'm doing a little research of my own," I said vaguely.

Laurel's brow wrinkled. "On ghosts? I would think you'd be an expert by now." She read the title aloud. *"A Girl's Guide to Ghosts and Their Spiritual Journeys."* She looked confused. "Is it chick lit or nonfiction?"

I closed the book and set it aside. "It's not helpful is what it is." I picked up another book from my secret stash and began to flip through it.

"A Good Ghost's Survival Guide? What are you trying to find?" Laurel asked.

I knew there was no way out now. I should've stuck to the original plan. I closed the book and blew out an anxious breath. "I'm worried about Gareth."

"Why? He seems to be making great progress with Lyra."

"Oh, he is." I slumped in my seat. "That's not what I'm worried about."

Laurel lowered her voice, even though there was no one in sight. "Then what is it?"

I fiddled with the quill on the table. "Gareth's ghost is trapped in Spellbound because of the curse. Those box tickers in the bureaucratic afterlife wouldn't let him enter another realm. If we break the curse, I worry about what will happen to him."

A flash of understanding lit up Laurel's eyes. "So if we break the curse, you're afraid Gareth will finally be able to pass into the next realm?"

I nodded. "I want to know whether he'll have a choice at that point. Will he simply evaporate and I'll never see him again?" I wasn't sure which realm vampires moved on to, but I was fairly certain it wouldn't be the same place I went.

Laurel appeared thoughtful. "What about the other residents who've died over the years? Their spirits aren't all trapped here."

"Not that we can see," I said. "I have a connection to Gareth because of the house and my sorceress skills." That was the prevailing view, anyway. I was still an enigma to many in town, including me.

"And everyone can see Raisa," Laurel said, appearing to understand.

"Yep. She's just that powerful, even in death." I shuddered. As much as I liked Raisa, those iron teeth were still enough to put me on edge.

Laurel sat quietly for a moment. Finally, she said, "We all love Gareth, Emma, but I think the priority has to be figuring out how to break the curse. With the unicorn horn, the coven has never been this close before."

"Oh, I agree," I said. "I want to be ready, that's all. If there's a way to save Gareth, I want to know what it is now, before it's too late."

Laurel bit her lip. "I hate to ask, but have you considered the fact that Gareth might not want to be saved?"

I clenched my teeth. "What do you mean?"

"I mean maybe he's ready to move on," she said. "I know he loves you and Magpie, but it doesn't mean he'd choose to stay here if given the option to go. He is, by definition, a restless spirit."

Now it was my turn to fall silent. Gareth wouldn't choose to leave us, would he? As annoying as his presence was at times, especially with my upcoming marriage, I still couldn't imagine life without him.

"That's a ridiculously large pile of books, even for you lot."

A sharp intake of breath escaped me. "Gareth, what are you doing here?" I placed my hands over the book so he couldn't read the title.

"You know the library is one of the places I can manifest," he said. "I didn't realize you were here until I saw you." He chuckled. "I managed to scare a woman in the Diseases aisle by sliding a few titles off the shelf. *A Healer's Guide to Syphilis* and *Fish Odor Syndrome and You.*"

"You're awful," I said.

He shrugged. "Who knows? Maybe she'll find them useful." He tried to peer over my shoulder. "Why are you hiding your book?"

I leaned my elbow casually on the table and twisted my body toward him. "I'm not hiding anything. Laurel and I are working on breaking the curse and we're not supposed to have any information in public."

"The coven wants everything hush-hush until we're further along," Laurel added. Although she couldn't see or hear Gareth, she could tell his approximate location based on my body language.

"It's no harm if I look," Gareth said. "Who am I going to tell?"

"The Grey sisters," I said pointedly.

"Do you not trust me?" He began to sulk. You haven't seen sulking until you've seen a vampire ghost do it with flare.

I softened. "Of course I trust you. But the coven only just allowed me to participate and I don't want to be the one that immediately breaks the circle of trust."

"Good point," Laurel said, with a slightly too much enthusiasm.

Gareth made a disappointed face. "Fine. I'll go haunt the Horror aisle. I'm sure someone will appreciate my presence there."

"I'll see you at home," I said.

I let him go, at least for now. Unfortunately, it was more important to keep my research a secret than to soothe Gareth's hurt feelings. Once I knew more, I'd share with him.

Until then, I wanted to keep what little information I had to myself.

Thanks to Richard's tip, the next day I headed over to Spell-bound High School to talk to Sean, the pixie's older brother. The bell rang to signal the end of the school day. As students streamed out the double doors, I stood on the sidewalk, marveling at the diversity. Wings, horns, tails, colorful skin—Spellbound was a true melting pot. Or a paranormal potpourri. I was never sure of the right analogy.

I waited for the last students to trickle out before entering the lobby. A woman with sparkling silver reading glasses sat behind a reception desk.

"Can I help you, miss?" she asked.

"Hi, I'm looking for Sean, the guidance counselor," I said.

She narrowed her eyes. "You look a little old to be a student here. Is he expecting you?"

I cleared my throat. "Thank you for your keen observation. As a matter of fact, I am a little old to be a student here. I need to speak with him about a private matter."

"I see." She gave one more cautious look before pointing down the long corridor. "Third door on the left."

"Thank you." I walked down the stretch of corridor until I reached the third door, where I noticed Sean's name on a plaque. I knocked and pressed my ear against the door to listen for a response. The marching band chose that moment to walk by and, even without their instruments blasting, it was too noisy to hear properly.

"Come in," a muffled voice said.

I opened the door to see a tearful dwarf seated in a chair opposite Sean. He looked like a much younger version of Deacon, the jeweler.

"I'm sorry," I said. "I didn't realize you were with a student. It's loud in the corridor."

"That's okay," the dwarf said, wiping his nose with a striped handkerchief. "I was about to go. I have chess now anyway."

Sean smiled. "Viktor is an excellent chess player."

"That's great," I said. "I'm partial to checkers, but only because I never learned chess."

Viktor gave me a shy smile before vacating his seat. "If you can master checkers, you can master chess. You should try it sometime."

"Thanks, maybe I will," I replied.

I waited for Viktor to close the door behind him before I spoke. "Is he okay?"

Sean rubbed his eyes, clearly tired after a long day. "Nothing I don't deal with on a regular basis."

"Teenage hormones?" I queried.

"I wish," Sean said. "That would be easier in some ways. This is more of an existential crisis."

I glanced at the closed door. "Your students are suffering from existential crises?" It seemed to me they should at least reach middle age before that happened.

"Think about it," he replied. "They're young with their whole future ahead of them. A future that can only unfold here in Spellbound."

Oh. Now I understood.

"That must be tough," I said, considering it from a younger paranormal's viewpoint. I could remember sitting in my classroom in sixth grade and counting the years until I graduated. Even then, I believed I could go anywhere. Do anything. Spellbound students didn't have the luxury of dreaming, which only strengthened my resolve to break the curse.

"So which one is yours?" Sean asked with a pleasant smile.

I balked. "Which one?"

"Which student?"

My eyes snapped open. "You think I'm old enough to have a child in high school?" I touched the top of my head. "Do you see grey hairs?" If so, I needed to color them before the wedding.

He quickly realized his mistake. "No, no. I assumed maybe a young stepmom or an involved aunt. We have a fair number of those."

That sounded better. I took Viktor's empty seat. "I'm Emma Hart."

His brow lifted. "You're the sorceress."

"That's right. I'm here to talk to you about your brother."

Sean's cheerful expression faded. "Are you working with the sheriff? Because I want answers about his death and I want them yesterday. I know my brother, and Seamus wasn't in any kind of trouble."

"I completely understand your frustration, Sean," I said. "His death must've come as a horrible shock."

"It did." Sean's gaze intensified. "So do you have any leads?"

"We're working on it," I said. "We're tracking possible suppliers of hemlock. If we can find the right one, maybe he or she can lead us to the killer." I figured this was enough information to placate him and keep him talking to me.

"I try not to think about the hemlock part," Sean said, shuddering. "It's too awful."

"His neighbor is concerned about the house sitting empty," I lied. "Do you know if you'll inherit it? I'm sure Tomlin would be relieved to know someone's moving in soon."

Sean nodded. "That's what I've been told. No surprise that Seamus didn't have a will and I'm his next of kin, so it's pretty straightforward."

"You're his older brother, right?" I asked.

"That's right. Three years older." He straightened his tie. "Typical birth order personalities. I was the high achiever and he was…not."

"I'm surprised your mother left the house to Seamus instead of you," I said.

Sean gritted his teeth. "She was always coddling him. She knew I could take care of myself, so she thought it was a way of helping Seamus get a wing up."

"Did that bother you?" I asked.

Sean drummed his fingers on the desk. "Not really. I expected it from my mother. I think it was half the reason Seamus had such a hard time taking care of himself. When my mother was alive, she always stepped in instead of letting him fail."

Another vote for tough love. Maxwell didn't seem to be alone in that regard.

"You disagreed with that approach, I take it."

Sean's wings crushed against the back of the chair. "I expressed my opinion often enough, to the point where my mother and I had to agree to not discuss it anymore. It was negatively impacting our relationship."

Ugh. It was terrible when family dynamics got out of hand.

"I hate to ask, but what happened to your father? No one's mentioned him."

"He died when I was ten," Sean replied. "My mother never remarried and we became her world. I think she sensed Seamus needed her more, at least back then. He was only seven when our dad died." He swallowed hard. "It became a habit, you know? Taking care of Seamus. Making sure he was okay all the time."

A role Leanne likely filled after Seamus's mother died, until it became too much for her.

"So you never made an effort to claim the house, or at least get half the value?" I asked.

His nose wrinkled. "No, of course not. I intended to honor my mother's wishes. I didn't agree with her, but it was her house to give."

"I guess that's the bright side of a dark situation," I said. "You get the house anyway."

"I hate to admit it, but it couldn't come at a better time, really," Sean said. "I was considering selling my house and getting something bigger. My wife is pregnant with our third and we're short on space."

"Congratulations," I said.

"Thanks. I'm sorry the baby will never get to meet Uncle Seamus," Sean said. He gripped a quill on his desk and squeezed. "I won't pretend he was the best uncle in the world, but he was our only extended family member on my side. He has memories...had memories of our mother that I didn't have because they had such a close relationship."

"As nice as Seamus was, is there anyone you can think of that may have had a score to settle with him?" I asked. Even though it didn't sound like the brothers were tight, Sean could still have been privy to certain information.

"I know he owed Maxwell money and I assume you've already spoken to Olaf," Sean said.

Ruh roh. This was the first I'd heard of Olaf. "Remind me who that is."

"The wizard," Sean said. "He owns The Black Hat."

I shook my head.

Sean groaned. "I can't believe no one has mentioned Olaf."

"Why would a wizard have a beef with your brother?"

"I heard about it from one of my students, so word got around," Sean said. "You'd be surprised how much these kids pick up in town. Anyway, my brother was known to gamble on occasion, and he recently lost a bet with Olaf."

"What kind of bet?"

"I don't know the nature of it, only that Seamus owed Olaf some pixie dust, but didn't pay up and Olaf was not a happy wizard."

Seamus failed to make good on a promise to a wizard? And then died from hemlock poisoning? Olaf suddenly moved to the top of my suspect list.

"I'll make sure Astrid knows about this," I said, assuming she didn't already.

A knock on the door interrupted our conversation. An elf appeared in the doorway, her eyes brimming with tears.

"Can I talk to you, please?" she asked, her voice scratchy from crying.

"Let me get out of your way," I said apologetically. "Thanks for your time, Sean." I gave the elf a pat on the shoulder as I passed her. "Don't worry," I said. "It'll get better. It always does."

CHAPTER 11

"WHAT'S THE SPECIAL TODAY?" I asked.

"Bucksberry fizz and caviar," Agnes replied.

"In your dreams," I shot back.

Agnes eyed me. "You could make it happen. One little flick of those sorceress fingers."

"Agnes." I used my warning tone to make it clear bucksberry fizz and caviar would not be on the menu today courtesy of me.

We made our way to the cafeteria of the care home where I'd promised to join her for lunch so we could discuss the coven's most recent findings. No sooner had I pushed open the double doors when a voice shrieked in horror.

"Watch out for the kittens!"

I whirled around, hoping to avoid whatever kitten calamity threatened to unfold. The floor around me was bare, however.

"Hazel's hallucinating again," Agnes whispered.

"Nothing wrong with my hearing, Agnes Weatherby," Hazel said. The elderly elf stood next to one of the long tables, which was currently empty. The lunch crowd hadn't quite meandered in yet. "And I am *not* hallucinating. There must be a hundred kittens on this floor. You're simply as blind as the bat you rode in on."

"I'm a witch," Agnes huffed. "We don't ride bats."

"I admit to having ridden one or two in my day," Hazel said. "Vampires are delightful creatures. Terribly sexy." She gestured wildly to my feet. "Watch it! You're on that little one's tail."

I gingerly lifted my foot so as not to crush the imaginary kitten.

"Aren't they the sweetest?" Hazel said, staring down at a kindle of adorable kittens only visible to her.

"I take it you had cats before you moved here," I said.

"Oh, yes," Hazel replied. "Witches aren't the only ones. Of course, mine can't talk to me the way familiars can, but I don't mind. We have our own ways of communicating."

"I'll bet," Agnes muttered.

I pretended to admire the kittens on the floor. "They're all lovely. Such beautiful eyes."

"Aren't they, though? I'm so grateful the care home allows pet companions." Hazel bent over to stroke one and I felt a pang of sympathy. While I understood the reasons why the care home didn't allow actual pets, I couldn't imagine severing such an important bond.

I cast a furtive glance around the cafeteria. "Let me know if you see anyone official," I said in a hushed tone to Agnes.

Her lips curled. "That was a quick one-eighty. Taking one for the team, are we?"

"Don't get excited," I said. "I'm not planning to make a habit of it." Besides, it would be a good test of my manifestation skills. If I could manifest kittens, maybe my mother's letters weren't far behind.

"Ditch the doubt," Agnes hissed. "I can feel it oozing out

of you. You're a sorceress, my dear. Don't be afraid to act like one."

I closed my eyes and gathered the magical energy into a ball in the pit of my stomach. Once I felt secure, I focused my will, stretched out my arms and said, "Hats, gloves, scarves, and mittens/cover this floor with adorable kittens."

I heard the sweet sound of purring before I even opened my eyes. There were kittens everywhere. Hazel was stooped over, laughing as the kittens licked her hands.

"They always lick me," the elf said. "They must like the taste of salty elf."

Even Agnes enjoyed the feline attention. She sat on the floor as the kittens piled on top of her, clamoring for attention.

"I'd like to see you get up from that position," I said.

The double doors opened and I inhaled sharply before relaxing again. "Welcome to Catty Corner, Silas."

The genie floated in, gobsmacked by the scene. "I'm tempted to point the finger at Agnes."

"Would I magic in a hundred kittens?" Agnes snapped.

"Too right," Silas said. He floated lower so he could pet as many kittens as his hands could reach. "It'd be frogs or snakes with you. Nothing cuddly."

"Why do you think I find you so appealing?" Agnes shot back.

Silas perked up. "Did my ears deceive me? Or did you just admit you find me appealing?"

"These kittens are distracting me from my usual bad temper," Agnes said.

Silas grinned. "Maybe we should have kittens here more often."

The doors opened again and Estella glided into the cafeteria in her magical wheelchair. The dwarf's look of glee was unmistakable. "Kittens!"

"I think they're a big hit," I said.

One of the cafeteria workers came out from behind the serving station to stroke the kittens' soft fur. "It's a health and safety violation, but I won't tell."

"Performing magic is also a care home violation," Estella said.

"They wouldn't dare ban Emma from coming here," Agnes said. "Or they'd have one ornery witch to contend with."

"And they'd have a riot on their hands," Silas said, giving me a wink. "She's our favorite visitor."

"Personally, I prefer that hunky Daniel," Hazel said, ensconced in kittens. "But I'd be disappointed about Emma, too."

"Emma's brought you kittens," Silas said. "How can she not trump the Harp Plucker?"

Hazel gave him a dismissive look. "What do you mean, you delusional old genie? These are *my* kittens."

No one bothered to correct her.

The clock struck twelve and more residents drifted into the cafeteria, eager to sample the day's options. They stopped short upon seeing a hundred kittens swarming the room.

"Is the giant stashing food under his bed again?" one of the elderly pixies asked.

My stomach churned at the thought.

"Someone needs to report him," her companion said. "We can't have his snacks running loose."

Note to self: locate the giant's room and sweep for kittens.

"I hate to break up the paw-ty," I said, "but I've got to send these kittens away before word gets around."

"I'll forgive you for that terrible pun because I'm holding a kitten," Agnes said. When she rubbed noses with one of the kittens, Silas's mouth dropped open.

"Can we do this again sometime?" he asked. "I rather like this side of her."

"You like all sides of me," Agnes said. "Or have you forgotten the other night?"

I smacked my forehead. Okay, definitely time to recall the kittens. I summoned my magic, focused my will and said, "No one will know, no one to blame/send these kittens from whence they came."

In the blink of an eye, the kittens were gone. There was a disappointed groan, except from Hazel, who continued to pet her hallucinatory kittens.

We grabbed trays and joined the line for food.

"Tell us about the wedding plans," Estella said. "Let us live vicariously through you."

"I think you should get married right here in the cafeteria," Silas said. "You can't do better than the lime gelatin dessert we've got."

"They don't want their guests to hate them," Agnes snapped. "There's enough of a line in town for that."

"Hey," I objected.

"Oh, don't worry," Agnes said. "It's more him than you. That angel did a lot of damage back in the day and memories are long."

"I rather like Daniel," Silas said. "He helped me improve my poker face. Turns out I had several tells."

"Don't worry," Agnes said, bumping him with her hip. "You still do."

"We're still making decisions about the reception," I said. "I'll let you know once I have more information."

"Give us an update on the curse then," Silas said, holding up his plate for another helping of meat.

I hesitated. "I'm meant to keep it within the coven."

"I'm in the coven," Agnes said. "You're telling me."

"I know, but I can't discuss it in front of the others," I said.

"Lady Weatherby...Sorry, Jacinda Ruth expressly forbade us from talking about it to outsiders."

Agnes's wrinkled brow gained a few more creases. "My friends here are very wise and have seen and done a lot in this world before they ended up here. Silas has had several run-ins with enchantresses."

Silas nodded solemnly. "If by run-ins, you mean sexual relations, then yes, I have."

Agnes groaned. "Keep your memories in your pants, Silas."

"I'll be ready to make new ones after lunch," he whispered in her ear.

I cringed. "Silas, would you mind terribly if I ate lunch with Agnes alone? As much as I agree with her about your... worldly experiences, I don't want to break my promise to the coven." I'd only just been invited to attend these meetings and I had no desire to be cast out.

"Fine, fine," he said, and floated away to join Hazel at a table. "Message received."

"I feel terrible," I said, once he was out of earshot.

"Don't," Agnes said. "I plan to tell him everything after you're gone anyway. You won't get blamed for that."

"Next time, don't tell me you plan to do that," I said. "Ignorance is best."

Agnes snorted. "Yes, that's your motto, isn't it?"

We sat at a smaller table by ourselves, as far away from the others as possible. I filled her in on all the information to date, including Laurel's interpretation of the symbols.

"Sounds like you're making real progress," Agnes said, chewing thoughtfully.

"Do you have any idea which coven members would have been working on breaking the curse and why they might have stopped?" We had no idea when the parchment was created or why it was hidden for so long.

"It has to predate me," Agnes said. "I never would've made witches and wizards hide their findings. I would've been thrilled to be head of the coven when the curse was broken. What a legacy."

"Do you have any concerns at all about breaking the curse?" I asked. "What it might mean for Spellbound?"

She licked her fingers. "More excitement than concern. Think of the liquor out there I haven't tried yet. And while I'm still young enough to enjoy it, too. Hot damn."

I laughed. I couldn't argue with her positive outlook.

"I think residents will be happy to have their freedom," I began, "but they're also worried about an influx of new paranormals. The town's entire infrastructure will need to be overhauled."

"One day at a time, my dear," Agnes said, patting my hand. "You have your mother's letters and a wedding to worry about right now. Guests with poor taste that want green gelatin. Don't let yourself get distracted. It's not up to you to solve the problem that's plagued us for years. This town has been closed off for a long time. A little while longer makes no difference to anyone."

Despite Agnes's wise words, I still felt a sense of responsibility that I couldn't explain. Then again, I'd always made a habit of taking on other people's problems, even in the human world. It was in my nature.

"You're right, Agnes," I said. "Breaking the curse is important, but so is my life. I manifested a hundred kittens today. A hundred!" I felt my resolve strengthen. "I'm bringing my mother's letters here, Agnes, one way or another. If anyone can do it, I can."

Agnes punched the air. "That's the spirit, my little sorceress. Even though you neglected to bring me a bottle of Goddess Bounty, I believe in you."

It may have taken some time, but, finally, I was beginning to believe in me, too.

The Black Hat was located on a side street not far from the library and the bank. It was a surprisingly dingy building for Spellbound. The exterior paint was noticeably chipped and one of the shutters hung crooked. I was tempted to whip out my wand and fix the shutter, but I stopped myself, wondering whether the look was deliberate. Some kind of magical shabby chic.

I pulled open the door and entered the shop. There was no sign of Olaf or anyone else for that matter. Music played softly in the background. The shelves were lined with books and accessories you would expect a magician in the human world to own—ropes, a large cage with white rabbits, coins, playing cards, throwing knives, and an assortment of capes.

I jumped back when a black cat shot out from underneath the table. He began meowing incessantly at my feet, demanding attention. I leaned down to scratch behind his ear and he purred.

"Aren't you friendly?" I said. What a far cry from Magpie.

"I see you've met Steve," a voice said.

I glanced up at a tall man wearing a black trench coat. He sported a five o'clock shadow and circles under his eyes so dark, they looked like bruises. Given that the temperature in Spellbound was constantly perfect, the trench coat seemed particularly out of place.

"You must be Olaf," I said, extending my hand. "I'm Emma Hart. I think we may have met at a coven event." That was a lie, of course. There was no way I wouldn't remember a wizard like Olaf. He stood out like a cactus in a rose garden.

"You're the sorceress," he said, giving me the once-over. "Funny, you don't look particularly powerful."

I stopped scratching the cat and rose to my full height. "That's why they say looks can be deceiving, I guess. To be honest, I'm not sure how powerful I really am. We're still in the figuring-it-out phase."

"So why would a sorceress be interested in a magician's tricks?" Olaf asked.

"Why would a wizard be interested in a magician's tricks?" I replied. It seemed to be a poor career choice, to expect to impress a town full of paranormals with illusions and magic tricks. It would be like trying to sell fins to mermaids.

"Wouldn't be the first time I've heard that," Olaf said. "I still book the odd party here and there. I figure one of these days, if the curse ever breaks, I'll be all set to make my way in the human world. They love this kind of stuff."

He produced a coin from behind his ear and handed it to me.

"That they do," I agreed. "But you're a wizard. You can use *actual* magic. Why use magicians tricks?"

"Because it's a challenge," he replied. "Real magic isn't challenging for me or any of the magic users in town. Creating the appearance of magic…" This time he produced a coin from behind my ear. "Now that's impressive work. I consider it to be art. I don't expect you to understand."

"You forget that I'm still new to magic," I said. "Believe me, I do understand." I could see why he suffered from gambling debts and a drug problem, if the rumors were true. He was struggling in his current environment. Spellbound wasn't the right place for a wizard like Olaf.

"I've been trying to keep my ear to the ground regarding the coven's efforts to break the curse," Olaf said. "Any chance you have inside information? I'm not the most popular wizard, so I tend to get left out of coven updates."

"The coven is working very hard on this," I assured him.

"Everyone has a stake in the outcome. Even those that intend to stay here will still want the option to travel, to see long-lost relatives, or visit new places."

"I guess you'd go running straight back to where you came from," Olaf said.

Steve jumped onto a nearby shelf, demanding more attention. "What makes you say that?" I asked.

"You may be a sorceress," he said, "but you've lived your whole life as a human. You must still be uncomfortable here. Mother Nature knows I've never fit in here. I can only imagine how you feel."

"That's the thing, Olaf," I said. "I never felt at home where I came from. Coming to Spellbound has been like coming home for the first time. I've met the most amazing friends and I'm engaged to the angel of my dreams. None of that would have happened if I'd stayed in Lemon Grove. I wasn't meant to be there. That's the way I look at it."

He gazed at me with interest. "Fascinating. Thank you for that."

I cocked my head. "For what?"

"For giving me hope," he said. "I want to believe there's somewhere I belong out there. Maybe one day I'll get the chance to find out."

I felt a rush of sympathy for the lost wizard. I understood how he felt, even though my own experience in Spellbound was very different from his. I was so distracted by our conversation that I nearly forgot the reason I was there.

"I understand you were friendly with Seamus," I said, getting to the point of my visit.

Olaf scowled. "Just one more reason to hate living here. One less friend who gets me."

"Was he a friend?" I asked. "I heard you had some kind of magical rivalry."

"We were always gambling against each other," he said.

"But it was nothing more than a friendly competition. Neither of us took our wins and losses personally."

"Yet you were angry with him recently, I understand," I said.

Recognition flickered in his dark eyes. "You mean the pixie dust incident."

"What happened? All I know is that Seamus lost a bet." Okay, I knew a little more than that, but it was better to let Olaf give me his version of events.

Steve switched his focus to Olaf and meowed.

"Yes, I think she's very nice, too," Olaf said. The wizard began to stroke the cat's back without taking his attention from me. "We were at the casino playing Wizard's Folly."

"Is that a card game?" I asked. The name was new to me.

"Yes, it's like Seven Card Stud, but more complicated," Olaf replied. "Anyway, we decided to up the ante at the last minute. If I lost, I had to reveal one of my magician secrets. You're from the human world. You know how valuable they are."

"Was Seamus interested in that?" I asked. It seemed to me a pixie would have no need for sleight-of-hand tricks when he had pixie dust.

"He thought it would be a bit of fun," Olaf said. "Something to entertain his nephews with." Olaf paused, and I got the sense that he was thinking about the family that Seamus left behind. "If I won, Seamus promised me a jar of pixie dust. I find it useful for certain spells. Plus, it's nice not to need a wand on occasion. I know your magic is more sophisticated than that, but most of ours isn't."

"And I take it you won the game," I said.

Olaf couldn't resist a proud smile. "It was a good night for me. I'm not usually that lucky. When I went to collect my winnings from Seamus the next day, he handed me the jar as agreed and I went on my way. It was only when I went to use it later on that I discovered it wasn't pixie dust at all."

I knew where this was going. "Coffee grounds?" I queried.

He gave me a sharp look. "How did you know that?"

"Because I know who did it."

"What do you mean 'who did it'? I thought Seamus did it as a prank on me. I was furious."

"It was a prank," I said, "but not by Seamus. It was his neighbor, Tomlin. He replaced the pixie dust with his own coffee grounds. They'd been arguing over a tree and it escalated."

Olaf appeared stunned by this revelation. "Seamus swore up and down he didn't do it, but I didn't believe him. I was so angry."

"Why were you so angry about it?" I asked. "It was harmless enough. Coffee grounds weren't going to hurt you."

Olaf hesitated. "I may not have been in my right mind when I attempted to use the pixie dust," he admitted.

"You mean you were already upset about something else?" I asked.

Olaf rolled his eyes. "For a human, you really are naïve. No, I mean I was literally not in my right mind."

Oh. He meant drugs. "Do you have access to a lot of illicit substances?"

Olaf's dark eyes widened. "Why do you ask? Are you interested? Because I have a couple of discreet sources."

"Can you get anything you want?" I asked. "Even things like hemlock and nightshade?"

Olaf rubbed his five o'clock shadow. "I've never asked for poisons myself. I can certainly find out if that's what you want."

He didn't seem to realize what I was asking. That only made me more certain of his innocence. Magical miscreant or not, Olaf was not our guy.

"That's okay, thanks. So did you work things out with Seamus?"

Olaf nodded. "I went back the next day and he gave me the real pixie dust. He apologized profusely. I was still bitter, but I let it go. Now I'm super glad I did. Life's too short, you know?"

It really was.

Steve rolled over onto his back so that Olaf could rub his belly. He reminded me more of a dog than a cat.

"I still can't believe Seamus is gone," Olaf said. "He was one of the few paranormals here who understood my struggle."

I offered a sympathetic smile. "Well, consider me Seamus's replacement because I really do understand, Olaf. You're not alone, even though it may feel that way at times. And if you ever want to talk, I'm happy to listen."

He perked up. "Would you tell me more about the human world? I hear there's this incredible place called Las Vegas. It sounds like bliss to me."

I laughed. "You'd have to ditch the trench coat," I said. "It's a city in the desert, and you would be way too overheated. I definitely think it's somewhere you'd enjoy, though."

His lips formed a satisfied smile. "Once again, Emma, you've given me hope. Thank you for that."

"We all need hope, Olaf," I said softly. "Sometimes it's the only thing that gets us through the day."

CHAPTER 12

"What's wrong, Emma?" Sophie asked.

The five remedial witches were in the secret lair, supposedly working on wards, although my mind was elsewhere.

I glanced up at Sophie, still lost in thought. "Huh?"

"For the luckiest girl in Spellbound, you look pretty unhappy," she said, coming to sit beside me. "Anything I can do?"

"I'm not unhappy," I replied, setting aside the voodoo doll of Lady Weatherby I was meant to be protecting with a ward. "I've been mulling over my last therapy session with Dr. Hall. She doesn't want me to get my hopes up about my biological mother."

"Is this to do with the letters?" Laurel asked.

I nodded. "If I get my hands on them again, I may not like what I find. All this time, I've been hoping the letters will tell me my mother missed me and wanted me back." My voice grew softer. "But what if they don't?"

Sophie placed an arm across my shoulders. "Emma, no matter what the letters say, they won't be a rejection of you.

Your biological mom never knew you. She never knew how amazing you'd grow up to be."

A tear slid down my cheek. "I'm so frustrated that I can't seem to do a simple manifestation spell. I'm supposed to have sorcery skills. Why is this so hard for me?"

"Have you considered the possibility that the letters have a protection spell to keep them in place?" Begonia asked, abandoning her voodoo doll to come and sit with us.

"Agnes and I have discussed the possibility," I said. "But there's no way to know for sure."

"It might be an emotional block," Laurel said. "You want these letters so badly, your magic has gone on the fritz."

That was an entirely plausible explanation. I seemed to manifest everything *except* the one item I truly wanted.

"What if we all helped you?" Begonia suggested. "What if the five of us channeled our will into you at the same time and gave you an extra magical boost? That might be enough to push past your emotional block or a protective spell, whatever the obstacle is."

"*E pluribus unum,*" I blurted, seized by a childhood memory.

"Latin, isn't it? Is that part of the spell?" Sophie asked.

"No," I said, with an embarrassed laugh. "It's something I learned in school. It was the motto of the original thirteen colonies in the U.S. when they decided to form one single nation. It means *out of many, one.*"

"What made you think of it now?" Laurel asked.

"I don't know. I guess because we're going to combine the power of all five of us into one magical burst." I glanced over my shoulder at Millie. "Will you join in?" She'd been sitting alone at the table, working on a chart of poisonous plants for extra credit, complete with illustrations.

"Let me finish this root system and I'll be right there," she said, her focus fixed on the chart. No one could ever accuse Millie of being lazy.

"Are you sure it's safe to try this here?" Sophie asked. "What if we blow up the secret lair or something?"

"I doubt we'll cause an explosion. Besides, the secret lair is probably safer than the care home," I replied. "There's no danger of anyone walking in on us and complaining about our use of magic." Thankfully, no one had reported the kitten incident.

Laurel rubbed her hands together. "This is great. Come on, Millie. I've been itching to work on more sophisticated magic."

"You've been too busy deciphering old parchments," Sophie said.

"And that's sophisticated in its own way," Begonia added.

"Come on, Millie," Laurel called. "We're ready."

Millie set down her quill and joined us around the coffee table. "Just because Lady Weatherby asked you to help with the secret project doesn't make you our boss."

"I wasn't trying to be your boss," Laurel replied. "I'm excited to try this. That's all."

"So I should do my usual manifestation spell?" I queried.

"Yes, except this time, we'll all hold hands and focus our will at the same time," Laurel said.

"It's a packet of letters, right?" Begonia asked.

I explained the letters in greater detail, including the place where I'd discovered them—in a box in my grandparents' old barn.

"Sounds good. Are we ready?" Begonia asked.

We positioned ourselves in a circle around the coffee table, clasped hands, and closed our eyes. I gave us a moment to focus our respective wills before I began the spell.

I took a deep breath, my stomach churning from nerves. As the witches' magic flowed into me, I gathered the energy in the pit of my stomach, same as when I manifested the kittens.

"Bring to me like ship to land/letters by my mother's hand."

I felt the energy shift. It was like a window opening and allowing in a slight breeze at first, followed quickly by a rush of air. I heard a few items topple over and papers flutter to the floor. When I dared to open my eyes, a familiar sight greeted me.

"The letters," I whispered.

Beside me, Begonia squealed with delight. "We did it!"

Emotions threatened to overwhelm me. We released hands and I stared at the packet on the coffee table, afraid to touch them.

"It worked," Millie said, sounding surprised.

"That was a good idea, Begonia," Laurel said.

"I do have them on occasion," Begonia said, and I detected a note of pride in her voice.

I barely heard the rest of the conversation around me. I was too focused on the letters. They were finally here in Spellbound. Maybe now I would get the answers I'd been dreaming of ever since I discovered the truth about my heritage.

"Well?" Millie prompted. "Are you going to stare at them all night or actually read them?"

I touched the letters to make sure they were real. The envelopes were thick and grainy. Definitely real.

"I think I'll take them home with me, if you don't mind. Now that I actually have them, I'm not quite ready." I'd probably wait for Daniel to be with me in case I needed emotional support. Not that the witches couldn't be supportive—they were incredible friends—but it was Daniel I wanted by my side.

"Let us know if you need us," Begonia said. "Send Sedgwick or even Gareth."

"I will," I promised. I tucked the letters into my cloak pocket. "Millie, would you mind flying me home?"

Millie's eyes bulged. "On my broomstick?"

I nodded. "I'd like to get there as quickly as possible."

Millie hesitated. "Are you sure that's wise? This is a new blouse." She smoothed the front of her white top.

"I took my anti-anxiety potion this morning," I said. "I should be okay." Although I felt queasy, it wasn't due to heights. I was anxious to be in the comfort of my own home with my mother's letters.

"Let's go then." Millie held out a hand and pulled me up from the sofa.

"Good luck, Emma," Sophie said. "We hope you find what you're looking for."

"Thanks, everyone," I said. So did I.

"How's my case coming along?" Tomlin asked. He sauntered into my office, appearing far more relaxed today than he had during previous conversations.

"I'm still hoping the Akers decide to talk Rochester into dropping the charges," I replied.

He scratched his cheek. "That's your strategy? Hope the Akers behave like decent paranormals? They're wereferrets. It isn't likely."

I wagged a finger at him. "Now that sounds like the Akers talking about a werelynx. Try to be the bigger paranormal."

Tomlin puffed out his chest. "Good point. So if they won't agree, then what?"

"Then I'll try to persuade Rochester. Sometimes he sees sense. Failing that, I'll prepare your case to go before the judge."

"A judge makes it all seem real," Tomlin said, a nervous edge creeping back into his voice.

"Don't worry, Tomlin," I said, adopting my most reassuring tone. "If we end up in court, I'll present a good defense."

"What will that be?" he asked.

"That you weren't aware you were on private property. There were no signs. No wards. No markings. The owners never spoke to you."

Tomlin arched an eyebrow. "And that will be enough?"

I shrugged. "I can't say for certain. I'll head out to the property once I know for certain we're trying the case and see if I can find any more supporting evidence. The more we have, the stronger your defense."

Tomlin nodded solemnly as Althea bustled into the room with a latte. She set the cup on my desk with a flourish.

"Your usual, Boss Lady," the Gorgon said.

"Thank you," I said and took a grateful sip. "You have no idea how badly I needed this."

From beneath her polka dot headscarf, the snakes hissed.

"Is that a new wrap?" I asked, inclining my head.

Althea touched the fabric. "It's one of Amanda's. The girls aren't sure how they feel about polka dots."

"It looks good," I said, and the snakes quieted. "Better than a napkin."

"I should hope so. I'll let you get back to business," Althea said. She sashayed back to her adjoining office.

"It must be nice to have someone wait on you like that," Tomlin said.

I laughed. "Wait on me? Althea?"

"Sure. She brings you lattes. Gets your paperwork ready. Schedules your appointments."

"That's her job," I said. "She gets paid, you know."

Tomlin looked wistfully at the door. "I miss Geena."

"You miss your relationship or you miss someone doing things for you?" I queried.

He offered a rueful smile. "Is it wrong to want both?"

It seemed to me that was part of the problem with his relationship. He was more than willing to take without offering something in return. The werelynx didn't seem to realize that relationships were a two-way street. Geena wanted him to bring something to the table. When he didn't, she bailed. If he didn't figure that out soon, he was doomed to repeat the same mistake in his next relationship.

"I don't mean to overstep," I began, "but have you ever considered therapy? I find it helpful to work through relationship issues with a professional, so that I don't repeat bad patterns."

"A professional what?" he scoffed. "Listener? I don't think anyone is more qualified to listen to me because of a few classes."

I cringed. "That's up to you, Tomlin. I happen to find it helpful, but therapy isn't for everyone." I would have loved to put him in a room with Dr. Hall and repeat his end of the conversation. She'd bust out her university degree and then give him a sharp kick in the solar plexus...if he was lucky.

"I heard you spoke to Sean," he said.

"That's right. How did you know?" I asked.

"He was at the house yesterday going through his brother's belongings."

"I guess he needs to pack everything up so his family can move in," I said. "I imagine they want to be settled before the baby's born."

Tomlin appeared blank. "He didn't have boxes. He was looking through Seamus's papers. I think he felt guilty about writing that letter and wanted to get rid of it."

Now it was my turn to look blank. "What letter?"

"He wrote Seamus a letter a while back, threatening to

sue him for the house," Tomlin said. "He got his wish, but at his brother's expense. That can't feel very good."

I gaped at Tomlin. "Did you see the letter?"

"Not this time around, but Seamus read it to me back when he got it," Tomlin said. "He was bummed. Sean wanted the house or half the value. Seamus knew he couldn't give him half. He didn't have that kind of money, but he also didn't want to fight with his brother about it. His mom hated when they fought."

Well, that certainly put Sean in a new light. He'd lied to me about intending to honor his mother's wishes.

"Did Sean find the letter?" I asked.

"I didn't stick around to find out," Tomlin said. "It seemed kinda personal. I only stopped by to see who was in the house. I wanted to make sure it wasn't a…"

"Trespasser?" I offered with a wry smile.

"Burglar," Tomlin finished.

"Thanks for coming in, Tomlin," I said. "This has been a very productive meeting." More than he realized.

I stood in front of the Grey sisters' cave, a heavy bag slung over my shoulder. It contained the usual treats for the trio—a headless chicken, a jug of Goddess Bounty, and a bar of chocolate.

"Come in, you will," Lyra said. She motioned for me to enter the mouth of the cave.

"I come bearing gifts," I said, and handed over the headless chicken at the first opportunity. Even in a bag, I didn't want to carry it any longer than necessary. Eating a nice grilled chicken and toting around a dead one were two very different activities.

"Something looks different," I said, as I followed her into the main living area of the cave.

"Tried to paint, we did," Petra said. "To brighten a dreary space."

I followed her gaze to the cave wall where smears of dark red paint were evident. "What happened?"

"Not enough lizard blood," Lyra replied. "But this chicken will do, it will." She shook the bag I'd given her.

My stomach turned over. "You used lizard blood as paint? Why not buy paint in town?"

Lyra exchanged glances with Petra, the sister currently sporting the eye. Even though Lyra now had a full set of eyes and teeth thanks to an agreement with me, Petra and Effie still shared an eye and a tooth between them.

"Shop we do not," Petra replied.

I could see how that would be difficult for Petra and Effie.

"You know what?" I said. "I bet I can conjure up paint with a spell. Would you like me to try?"

The sisters nodded.

A garden-variety coven spell was probably best for a job like this one. I produced my wand and focused my will. "Fix these walls before I faint/cover them all in bright red paint."

A collective gasp escaped the sisters, but I felt like I needed to vomit. In hindsight, red was not a good choice. Their cave was intimidating enough on a normal day. Now it looked like the well-used home of a serial killer...or a trio of serial killers.

"I don't know how I feel about the murder chic ambience," I said. "Let's try a different shade." I extended my wand and said, "I thank the Greys for being so mellow/change these walls to the color yellow."

The red walls shimmered and faded, replaced by a cheerful shade of yellow.

"Like it very much, we do," Effie said.

I tucked away my wand and wiped my brow. "Well, that's a relief. I have to admit, it really brightens up the place."

Usually the cave was dark and depressing. Now that Lyra had improved vision, it seemed only fair to spruce up their home. Next time I'd bring a plant instead of a chicken. Althea would approve.

Effie tried to take the eye from Petra, but the shorter sister refused to hand it over. Effie focused her blank face on me, an image that was always unsettling.

"Dreams, you have had," she said. "They cling to you like pixie dust."

"I have had an active dream life recently," I admitted. "Mostly strange and sometimes scary."

"Changes are afoot," Effie said. She gripped my arm and squeezed. "Changes within you."

I shook her off. "That's sort of the reason I'm here." I sat on a nearby boulder and tried to make myself comfortable. "I'm not sure if you've heard the news, but Daniel and I are getting married."

Excited chatter erupted as the sisters began to circle me.

"How lucky he is," Effie said.

"A catch," Petra said.

"The dream girl, you are," Lyra added.

I clutched my chest. "Stop it. You don't need to flatter me. I know *I'm* the lucky one."

The sisters' chatter halted abruptly.

"Know your worth," Lyra snapped, deviating from her usual singsong voice. "The angel has much and more to be grateful for, he does."

I straightened on the boulder. "I know my worth. I don't think he's better than me or anything like that."

The sisters' silence suggested otherwise.

"I mean, he *is* an angel and I'm just a…a sorceress learning the ropes…"

"*Just* a sorceress?" Petra echoed. Her one eye blinked at her sisters.

"Your worth has been proven," Effie said. "His remains uncertain."

I waved my hands emphatically. "No, no. You've got him all wrong. Daniel is a changed angel. He's worked hard to atone and make amends for past wrongs."

"Deserve you, does he?" Lyra asked.

"Yes," I said firmly. "One hundred percent. Not a shred of doubt in my mind." I paused. "But I thank you all for thinking so highly of me. It means a lot."

"Work with Gareth, I will," Lyra said. "He must attend all events."

I smiled. "Please do. My special day wouldn't be the same without him." I inhaled deeply. "While we're on the subject of my special day, I'd like to ask a favor. That's the reason I'm here."

The trio stopped circling me, which was helpful because I'd started to feel dizzy.

"Bridesmaids?" Petra asked hopefully.

I gulped. "Um, no. I'm sorry. I wish I had room for more. Actually, I was hoping you would..."

"Take pictures?" Effie interjected. "Use the eye, I shall, and promise to capture images in the magical box."

Oh boy. "No. I'm sorry. Miranda's going to take the wedding pictures," I said. The older Gorgon was a talented photographer. "That's Althea's gift to us."

The sisters crossed their arms and huffed in unison.

"I need ushers," I said.

"Ushers?" Effie repeated.

"To show guests to their seats for the ceremony," I said. "You'll get to wear special matching outfits and corsages. Daniel and I will pay for everything."

It had taken Daniel and I ages to come up with a reasonable task for the Grey sisters. The simple fact remained that many in Spellbound were terrified of the trio. If we used them to direct guests to their seats, no one would risk getting out of hand during the ceremony. They'd be bouncers in disguise.

The Grey sisters made encouraging sounds. Lyra placed her hands on my shoulders and kissed my cheek. The move was so unexpected and, quite frankly, a little gross from a woman who voluntarily smeared lizard blood on her wall, that I hopped in my seat.

"Honor us all, you do," she said.

"You're my friends," I said. "I want you to be a part of our day."

"What of Agnes?" Petra asked.

"Daniel and I are still discussing her role," I said, mainly because Daniel was reluctant to give Agnes any role at all. He was afraid she'd perform an itching curse on the guests or worse. "I'd like her to give a speech, but only if she promises to keep it clean."

"Then keep her away from alcohol, you will," Lyra grumbled.

"Ha! I'm not risking life and limb on my wedding day," I said. "I'll leave Lady Weatherby in charge of restraining her mother." And even that was a risk.

"Many thanks to you," Petra said. "We look forward to it, we do."

"Me, too," I said, beaming. "More than I've ever looked forward to anything in my life."

CHAPTER 13

THE FRONT LAWN of the high school was teeming with students. No one seemed eager to head straight home after school. A group of paranormals tossed a ball back and forth until a vampire sank his fangs into the ball and deflated it.

"Not again, Kevin," a fairy yelled in a voice typically reserved for put-upon mothers.

Kevin laughed and held up the ball so that the fairy could mend it with magic. They carried on playing as though nothing had happened.

I strode into the school and bypassed the receptionist. Thankfully, she was busy discussing recipes with a few other women and didn't register my presence. I spotted the pixie I wanted up ahead and raced to catch up to him.

"Why didn't you tell me about the letter, Sean?" I hustled to fall in step beside him as he sauntered down the corridor toward the teachers' lounge. Despite his pixie wings, he seemed perfectly content to walk instead of fly.

He kept his gaze locked on the corridor. "I don't know what you mean."

"The letter you sent to your brother, demanding the house or half the value. Sound familiar?"

He shushed me before coming to a dead stop in the middle of the corridor. Marching band students flooded us as he turned his attention to me. "The letter was a mistake, okay? I regretted it the moment I sent it."

"Then why didn't you tell me about it?" I demanded. "You said you intended to honor your mother's wishes. That was a lie."

"No, it wasn't." He pulled me into a nearby empty classroom and closed the door. "I knew how it would look if I told you the truth. I didn't even want to send the letter. It was my wife's idea. Pomona hated that Seamus got the house. She thought it was unfair." He raked an agitated hand through his hair. "And it was unfair, but I had no interest in fighting over the house."

"Then why pick one? You could have refused."

"I never intended to follow through with it," Sean said. "I only did the initial letter to satisfy Pomona."

"She never asked what the outcome was?" I queried.

"Oh, she asked," Sean said. "But I was always able to delay a real answer."

I folded my arms and fixed him with my hard stare. "Well, I guess she's happy now."

He seemed genuinely upset. "Of course not. No one is. Seamus was a decent pixie and Pomona feels guilty about the letter."

"Is that why you went to retrieve it from the house?" I asked.

Sean nodded. "We knew it would make me look bad and we didn't want anything to distract the sheriff from the real culprit."

"The better move would have been to tell us about the letter rather than hide it," I said. "Now you seem like you have something to hide. I bet one of your students could get you access to hemlock if you wanted it."

Sean shuddered at the mention of hemlock. "He didn't deserve to die like that. Hemlock is a terrible way to go."

"If it's any consolation," I said, "it sounds like he went pretty quickly according to Tomlin. And at least he wasn't alone when he died. I know it isn't much." But it was something.

Sean nodded, his lips twitching. He was close to tears. "Seamus was my little brother. I feel like I failed him. I spend time with these students every day, trying to make a difference in each of their lives. But how can I be successful at my job when I couldn't even save my own brother?" He broke down and began to cry.

"Your brother was murdered, Sean," I said, giving his arm a sympathetic squeeze. "How could you have saved him?"

"If I could have persuaded him to be more proactive," Sean blubbered. "More focused. I've never had any issues with staying the course. I was his older brother, for Nature's sake. I should have offered more guidance."

"That comes down to personality a lot of times," I said. "Even if you had done those things, Seamus was still Seamus. You can't blame yourself."

The classroom door flew open and a pregnant pixie fluttered there, looking ready to spit nails at the sight of another woman's hand on her husband's arm. "Sean, what exactly are you doing? You were supposed to meet me out front five minutes ago."

He took a step back from me. "Pomona, this is Emma Hart. She's investigating Seamus's death."

Pomona's anger faded. "Oh. I'm sorry I came charging in here. That's pregnancy hormones for you."

"That's okay," I said. "I understand."

Her gaze settled on my ring finger. "That's a beautiful ring."

"Thank you," I replied. "I'm still getting used to wearing it."

Pomona held up a naked finger. "My fingers are like fat sausages thanks to water retention, so my ring is safely in a warded drawer so the boys can't get to it. The last thing I need is to rush one of them to the healer for swallowing a diamond."

"Our boys are very oral," Sean added.

Pomona seemed to notice the tears in her husband's eyes for the first time. "Are you okay, Sean? Dear gods. Did they find out who did it? Is that why Emma's here?"

"Unfortunately not," he said, wiping the tears from his cheeks. "Emma came to ask me about the letter. She knew I took it from Seamus's house."

Pomona closed her eyes for a moment, realizing the enormity of the situation. "I made him write it. He didn't want to." She rushed to her husband's side. "You're not here to arrest him, are you? I know how it must look, but, I swear, he's innocent."

"I believe you," I replied. Based on everything I'd seen and heard, I had no doubt Sean wasn't the killer. "I only needed to clear up a misunderstanding."

"But you're no closer to finding the murderer, are you?" Sean asked, his disappointment evident.

"Not yet, but we will, Sean," I said soothingly. "It may take a little time, but we'll get there in the end. We always do."

After much persuasion, I finally convinced Daniel to agree to dinner with Begonia and Demetrius. Although I knew Demetrius wasn't his favorite paranormal, Dem and Begonia were serious now and I wanted the four of us to be able to go out together.

Due to the special occasion, Demetrius suggested the Secret Garden. It was one of the more upscale restaurants in town, so it seemed an appropriate choice.

"Emma tells me Spelled Ink is coming along nicely," Daniel said.

We sat at a square table overlooking the courtyard garden. It was an ideal spot to paranormal watch as well as admire the vibrant plants and flowers.

Begonia could barely contain her excitement. "Other than your wedding, I haven't been this enthusiastic about anything in ages."

Demetrius clutched his heart in mock agony. "Ouch."

She looked horrified. "I didn't mean to suggest…"

He chuckled. "I'm teasing you, my love. You don't need to stroke my ego."

"That's right," Daniel said. "Demetrius does it often enough by himself."

I kicked Daniel under the table and he stifled a groan.

Demetrius took Daniel's barb in stride. "The food is amazing here. I've never been disappointed."

"Maybe they could cater your wedding," Begonia suggested.

"That's part of the problem," I said. "We want to hire everywhere in town, but it's only one wedding."

"What about having the reception at the Mayor's Mansion?" Demetrius said. "Paranormals used to hold events there, although Mayor Knightsbridge had clamped down on it in recent years. Now that she's gone, it might be time to revisit the idea."

The Mayor's Mansion was a gorgeous building and I knew Lucy would respond favorably. "That's a great idea, Dem. We'll have to think about it."

"Do you know anything about your parents' wedding?" Begonia asked. "Any customs or traditions?" She leaned forward, her eyes glittering. "Do the letters say whether your biological parents were married? It would be wonderful if you could incorporate something from both."

"I don't know," I replied. "I haven't read the letters yet."

Begonia flew back against her chair. "What do you mean you haven't read them yet?"

Daniel placed a comforting hand over mine. "She's taking her time."

Begonia seemed to grasp the situation. "That's understandable. I'm sure it's quite scary."

"If you want an impartial third party to read them first," Demetrius said, "I'm happy to oblige. I can prepare you for the contents."

"Thanks, Dem. That's sweet of you, but I just need Daniel next to me and a cup of tea. Then I'll be ready."

"That can be arranged," Daniel said. "You only need to say the word."

"I know." I speared a piece of asparagus and shoved it into my mouth. I didn't want to have to defend myself.

"Your fear is natural, Emma," Demetrius said. "Everyone fears change to one degree or another. It's whether we push through the fear and don't let it dictate our behavior that matters."

"What makes you think it's a fear of change?" Daniel asked.

"Because whatever information is included in those letters threatens to change Emma's perception of her mother," Demetrius explained. "It might even change her understanding of her adoptive parents. What if the letters say that her biological mother wanted a relationship with her, but the adoptive parents refused? That type of knowledge would color Emma's view of the Harts forever."

My gut twisted. "I hadn't even considered that possibility. I've been more concerned about the reason my mother gave me up."

Demetrius appeared contrite. "I'm terribly sorry, Emma. I wasn't trying to put negative ideas into your head."

"No worries, Dem," I replied. "And you're right about my fear of change. I do think it's interfering with my ability to move forward. That's why the letters are sitting there unopened."

"I bet Gareth reads them when you're not home," Daniel said.

My jaw unhinged. "He would never!"

Daniel laughed. "I'm kidding. Of course he wouldn't. Gareth is the most trustworthy vampire I know, even when he was alive...or at least not dead undead."

The server stopped by the table to inquire about our meals.

"My compliments to the chef," Demetrius said. "I haven't had borscht this good in..." He stroked his chin, thinking. "Let's just say before I came to Spellbound."

"Geena will be pleased to hear it," the server said. "I know she took ages getting the recipe right. She's a real perfectionist."

"I hate to ask, but do you think she'd share the recipe?" Demetrius asked. "I'd love to make it at home sometime."

Begonia's eyes lit up. "That's a terrific idea."

"I'll see what I can do." The server retreated to the kitchen with the plates that had been scraped clean.

"So I have an idea for Daniel's bachelor party if anyone's interested," I announced.

"Does it involve a succubus and pompoms?" Demetrius asked.

Begonia elbowed him gently. "That sounds very specific."

Daniel grinned encouragingly. "Let's hear it then."

"How about a magician?" I asked.

No one responded.

"A magician can do all sorts of tricks," I continued. "Olaf's a master illusionist. He'd be great entertainment."

Daniel and Demetrius exchanged frowns.

"Do you want to address this one or shall I do it?" Demetrius asked him.

Daniel cleared his throat. "Emma, darling, as much as I love that you're thinking about my bachelor party and clearly thinking about how to help some magician realize his dreams, I'm not sure magic tricks make sense when entertaining a group of magic users."

"You're an angel," I said. "You don't perform magic. And Demetrius is a vampire."

"Yes, but we won't be the only two there," Daniel said. "And magic or no magic, I do have enviable skills."

"But Olaf makes things appear magical without actually using magic," I protested. "That's a real skill."

Daniel straightened. "Are you suggesting that flying is *not* a real skill?"

"Not at all," I replied. *It's just not one that I enjoy.* "Except you have wings. It's kind of obvious why you can soar majestically through the air."

Daniel cocked an eyebrow. "Majestically, huh?"

"I'll tell you what, Emma," Demetrius said. "I'm going to help out with Daniel's party. I'll see how I can incorporate some of Olaf's…magic."

Daniel appeared shocked. "You are? Why would you do that?" I understood his surprise. Daniel and Demetrius weren't exactly the best of friends.

Demetrius shrugged. "What kind of vampire would I be if I didn't step in to organize an incredible all-nighter?"

My eyebrows shot up. "An all-nighter? Is that necessary?"

Everyone laughed.

"Not necessary," Demetrius said with a wink. "But very, very fun."

I spotted the chef as she emerged from the kitchen and headed straight to our table. She was a slight woman of average height—her most noticeable quality was the huge smile plastered across her face.

"Hi, I'm Geena," she said. "Monique said you asked about my borscht recipe."

Demetrius grinned and I caught a glimpse of his impressive fangs. "It's honestly the best thing I've tasted in decades." He stopped and brushed a finger lightly against Begonia's cheek. "Present company excepted."

"Thank you so much. That's a huge compliment," Geena said. "I take great pride in my recipes."

"As you should," Demetrius said.

Geena fixed her attention on me. "I understand you've got your work cut out for you with my ex."

I blinked. "Your ex?"

"Tomlin, my ex-boyfriend," she said. "Someone told me you're representing him in a trespassing case."

I suddenly realized why her name sounded familiar. "Yes, I am. It's all a big misunderstanding, though. He was just scavenging for vegetables for a stew."

Geena burst into laughter. "Tomlin? Cooking a stew?"

"That's right," I said. "Now I understand why he didn't know how to make anything. With a cook like you in the house, it would've been a wasted effort."

She folded her arms and gave a crisp nod. "The kitchen was my domain. Tomlin just got in the way. He didn't know parsley from oregano. It was too distracting to have him there, constantly asking questions."

Her attitude reminded me of my grandmother. I wasn't allowed near the kitchen when she was cooking. Too much of a hindrance in her eyes, whereas I would have loved to have helped.

"He knows how to cook now," I said. "He's been working hard to teach himself. It seems like he took your…departure hard and has been trying to find productive ways to work through his grief. Apparently learning to cook has been a helpful distraction."

Geena's expression mellowed. "So he's managed to climb out of his funk?" Her voice softened. "Good for him."

"Was he in a funk when you were still together?" I asked quietly. I didn't want the nearby patrons to overhear us, but I was eager to get more information about my client. Maybe Geena could tell me something useful for Tomlin's defense.

"Not in the beginning," she said. "It happened gradually. He wouldn't want to do chores around the house. He seemed perpetually irritated by me. He said I made him feel like he couldn't do anything right. And maybe I was a little hard on him, but our temperaments are so different. It never would've worked out between us in the long run."

"And then you met someone else?" I asked.

She chewed her lip. "He's the sous chef here. We've known each other for years, but he knew I was in a relationship with Tomlin so he never expressed his feelings."

"Until he did," I said.

"I'd been upset over Tomlin's refusal to step up," Geena said. "I was fed up with pushing for change and hitting a brick wall. Lamar said Tomlin was a fool not to put in the work. That I was worth every ounce of effort." Her cheeks grew flushed. "I felt guilty for falling out of love with Tomlin, but Lamar and I truly are right for each other."

Begonia sighed happily. "I love a happy ending."

"Not such a happy ending for Tomlin," Daniel murmured.

"Tomlin's moving on," I said. "He worked out his dispute

with Seamus before he died. He's learning to cook and take care of himself." I wiped my mouth with the napkin and set it on the table. "He's excited about the future for the first time in a while."

"I'm glad for him," Geena said. "I hope he meets someone special. Everyone deserves a second chance."

Under the table, Daniel's hand grasped my knee and butterflies invaded my stomach. "I wholeheartedly agree," he said.

"If you promise not to share the recipe," Geena began, "I'll give it to you right now."

Demetrius's fangs protruded and he held up his wrist. "I'm happy to make a blood oath."

Geena waved him off. "No, no. Health and safety will be all over me in a heartbeat. Your word is good enough."

Demetrius retracted his fangs. "Then I give you my word."

CHAPTER 14

"Do you think it's weird that I asked Daniel to have a magician at his bachelor party?" I asked. "He didn't seem very excited about it."

"Don't ask me. I think most of what you do is weird," Gareth replied.

"Says the vampire ghost watching me shave my legs." I was seated on the edge of the bathtub in underpants and a T-shirt, running a razor down my legs.

He shrugged. "You know those legs don't interest me, nice as they are."

I carried on shaving. "I think it would be a boost to Olaf's ego if he could show off his skills. Maybe he'll climb out of his drug-addled stupor."

Gareth groaned. "Since when is Olaf on Emma's Over-sized List of Sympathetic Creatures?"

"Since I met him," I said. "He's a very nice wizard who feels out of place in this world. You of all paranormals should understand that."

"You don't have to appoint yourself the personal liaison to happiness," Gareth said.

"You make it sound like it's a bad thing," I snapped. "I didn't hear you groaning when I accepted responsibility for Magpie. And he doesn't even like me." I didn't mention the trust I was researching. I thought it might depress Gareth to contemplate Magpie's fate without me.

"That's different," Gareth sputtered. "He's a magnificent creature and deserves every advantage in life."

"Magnificent is one word for him," I muttered.

Gareth took a sudden interest in the floor tiles. "I do wonder if maybe your inclination to be sympathetic is what's at the heart of your relationship with the Winged Wonder."

I burst out laughing. "You think I fell in love with Daniel because I felt sorry for him? That's ridiculous."

"Let's be honest. He's a bit of an Eeyore, isn't he?" Gareth said.

"He went through a downbeat phase," I admitted, "but he's in a much better place now. Volunteering and making amends for past actions have made an enormous difference to his outlook on life."

"And you," Gareth added. "You can't omit the most important factor."

"Do you have any thoughts about the reception?" I asked. "We could try to have it at Swan Lake, but that would be a huge undertaking because of the food."

"You liked Markos's new place, didn't you?" Gareth asked. "The one with the maze."

"Tiki Bar," I said. "Yes, it's very nice." I smiled at him. "You just want an excuse to admire Markos in a suit."

"I don't need an excuse," Gareth objected. "I'm a ghost, remember? I can stalk him to my heart's content."

"That's not something I would advertise."

"Speaking of advertising, it would give the Tiki Bar a big boost, hosting a high-profile event. Markos would love you for it." He hesitated. "Then again, he already loved you so…"

"Stop it. He does *not* love me. And I think the Tiki Bar is a great idea. I'll make an appointment for Daniel and I to go over there and check out the catering menu." I nicked the skin near my ankle and blood trickled out. "I hate when I do that."

"Don't feel like you have to follow through with it," Gareth said.

"Go through with what?" I glanced down at my partially shaved legs. "I'll look silly with stubble on half my legs."

He waved me off. "By the devil, no. Shaving those legs is an absolute necessity. I'm surprised you haven't been mistaken for a shifter. I'm talking about the wedding."

I stopped shaving and peered up at him. "Wait, what? Why would I not go through with the wedding?"

"I don't know," he replied. "All sorts of reasons. Maybe you tell me I'm right and that you're only with him out of pity. You woke up one day and realized you didn't like the way he slurped his tea. You decide you can't possibly abide another fifty years of it."

I rinsed off the blood and resumed sliding the razor down my leg. "Daniel doesn't slurp his tea."

"You're missing the point. I only mean to say that if you decide to do a runner, I'll have Sigmund ready and waiting. I should be able to manage a car by then. I've been practicing when you're asleep."

"That...worries me," I said. "Please don't drive my car."

"It might come in handy at some point," Gareth said. "Besides, your car is so different from the jalopies here. Quinty did an excellent job adapting it."

"And, in case you've forgotten, Daniel was the one who had Sigmund pulled from Swan Lake and asked Quinty to adapt it for Spellbound," I said. "He's always been thoughtful and sweet, since the moment I met him."

Gareth grumbled to himself, unable to drum up a decent

argument. "Just bear it in mind. If you want to go, I'll help you."

I laughed. "And where would I go? The other side of town? This is Spellbound, remember?"

He crossed his arms and gave me a petulant look. "I'm your best friend. I care about your well-being."

I finished the last patch of skin and rinsed off my legs. "I appreciate the sentiment, but you know perfectly well that Daniel and I love each other. If two beings were ever destined to be together, it was us. I've never been more sure of anything in my life. This wedding *will* happen and I couldn't be happier about it."

Magpie stalked into the bathroom like he had every right to invade my privacy, his tail swishing left and right.

"Can I just remind both of you that we're in a bathroom?" I said pointedly.

"I know. I can see the loo right there," Gareth said. "I'm dead, not blind."

I shook my head. "You're insufferable."

"But you couldn't do without me."

Magpie inspected the small puddles of water on the floor before deciding he had no interest in hanging out with us in the bathroom. Smart hellbeast.

"Are you worried about that?" I asked. "That I'll be married and suddenly able to do without you?" I toweled off my legs and moved into the bedroom to put on a pair of khaki capris.

"I'm more worried about the poor excuse for pants you're wearing," he said.

I glanced down at my capris. "I wear these all the time."

"Not your trousers. Your pants."

"My pantaloons?" I joked. "Who doesn't love a big yellow smiley face on their butt?"

He glared at me. "You'll need to wear something a bit

more appealing for your future husband, don't you think? Those underpants are hideous."

I slipped on my shoes. "One minute you're driving the getaway car and the next minute you're offering advice on my intimate apparel? Make up your mind."

Gareth shuddered. "Forget I said anything."

"About my sex clothes?" I said. "I've already forgotten."

He groaned and disappeared from the room without another word and I couldn't resist a smile. At least now I knew a surefire way to get privacy when I needed it.

My hands trembled as I laid the letters neatly across the dining room table.

"Are you going to keep rearranging them or actually read them?" Gareth asked. He paced the length of the dining room, inasmuch as a ghost could pace.

"They need to be in date order," I said. "I don't want to accidentally read them out of order and misunderstand something."

"You're being absurd," Gareth said.

"Hey, I'm not the one who alphabetizes the spices," I said pointedly.

"That's different," Gareth shot back. "Alphabetical order is completely rational. This is procrastination, plain and simple."

The wind chimes sounded. "Daniel," I exclaimed, and hurried to the foyer.

"Why does he still feel the need to ring the bell?" Gareth asked testily. "He's here all the time as it is."

"He does it out of respect for you," I called over my shoulder. I yanked open the door and greeted Daniel with an enthusiastic kiss.

"If I knew I was going to get a greeting like that, I'd have come sooner." He tucked in his wings and stepped through the doorway. "Are you all set?"

Although I was nervous, I was determined to push through the fear like Demetrius suggested. "Let's do this."

When we returned to the room, the letters were scattered all over the floor. Magpie stood in the middle of the table, meowing angrily.

"He grew tired of waiting," Gareth explained.

I hurried around the room, collecting the letters and smoothing them flat. "Magpie, that was very rude. This is a huge moment for me. I don't want to be rushed." I picked up the last letter and gulped down air. "The truth is, I'm terrified." Tears pricked my eyes.

Daniel crossed the room and wrapped his arms around me. His white wings tickled my bare skin. "Demetrius was right. It's natural to feel this way."

I pulled a tissue from my pocket and wiped my nose. "I wish Demetrius could be with us to hear you say that. Talk about a defining moment."

"My jabs at Demetrius are out of habit," Daniel said. "I promise to make a genuine effort with him. It's clear he cares about you and how can I blame him?"

"He cares about me, but he loves Begonia," I said. "Try to remember that." I glanced at the letters in my hand. "What if she hated me? What if she wanted nothing to do with me?" All my doubts came crashing down on me at once.

Daniel kissed my forehead. "Impossible. Seriously."

"Elsa hated me," I argued.

"She had a reason," he said. "Not a good one, I admit, but she did have one. Your mother didn't hate you. You were a baby. An innocent. A piece of her soul."

I nodded, fighting an onslaught of tears. "Will you sit with me while I read them?"

"Of course," he said, and took my free hand.

"I will, too," Gareth said, floating behind us as we walked into the living room.

"Gareth says he will, too," I repeated.

"Do you mind, Emma, or would you rather he sit this one out?" Daniel asked.

Gareth didn't give me a chance to answer. "Of course she doesn't mind. I'm her best friend. She tells me everything."

"I don't tell you *everything*," I said.

Daniel glanced at me. "You tell him everything?"

"Can we keep the focus where it belongs?" I asked. "Gareth can stay as long as he's quiet." I sat on the sofa, clutching the letters like they might disintegrate at any moment.

Daniel draped an arm around my shoulders. "Whenever you're ready."

I plucked the first letter from the packet and opened it. It felt strange to see my mother's handwriting. The writing was long and expressive, full of character. She would not have won any penmanship awards from Mrs. Roberts, my fifth grade teacher. Mrs. Roberts liked each letter perfectly formed and between the provided parallel lines. There was no room for individual flourishes.

"Dearest Geri and Barron," I read aloud. "I hope this letter finds you both well. I inquire after the blood of my blood in the hope that you will take pity on a wretched soul and ease my suffering. Please tell me that all is as it should be. Signed, B."

"That's promising," Daniel said. "She wanted to know that you were okay. That's not written by a woman who doesn't care."

I was inclined to agree. It *was* a good start.

"Maybe there'll even be information about your father," Daniel said hopefully.

"I don't want to expect too much," I said. "But I like the way you think."

"Next one?"

I nodded as I opened the next letter. "Dearest Geri and Barron, I am most anxious to hear news of my progeny. Your silence is vexing, to say the least. How is she progressing? On good days, I imagine her with my most favorable features. On bad days, I imagine her with her father's soul, but then I relent and wish for his smile. Conflicted. Always conflicted. Dark days lie ahead, good witch, and I urge you to take every precaution. Signed, B."

"Dark days lie ahead," Daniel echoed. "So maybe you were right. Maybe you were sent away to keep you safe."

"But why? And why was I unsafe? Because of something my mother did or who she was?"

"Or who your father was," Daniel added. "That part about his soul is interesting."

The letters were generating more questions than answers. "Should I keep reading?"

"If you feel comfortable," he replied.

"Honestly, I keep getting lost in the fact that my mother held this paper. Formed these words on the page." I traced a few inky letters with my finger. "So far, they've been short and sweet. She asks questions with no indication as to whether she ever got answers."

"Do you think the Harts ever replied to her?" Daniel asked.

"It's hard to tell," I said. "Most of the time, she sounds like she doesn't expect an answer. It's like she's talking out loud to herself, wondering about me and sharing a little bit of her life." I reviewed a couple more letters. "She's traveled a lot in the U.S., but mostly places I've never heard of. Starry Hollow, Demonsback, Forked Tongue…The list goes on."

Daniel peered over my shoulder. "Those are paranormal

towns. No wonder you've never heard of them. Starry Hollow is off the coast of North Carolina and Demonsback is in Minnesota. I'm pretty sure Forked Tongue is in Arizona."

I continued to read. "Hey, this one has new information. What's a Warden of the West?"

"She mentions the Warden of the West?" Daniel asked, trying to find the passage. "Does she mention running from the law? That would explain why she gave you up. And where you inherited those troublemaking genes." He rubbed my thigh to show me he was only kidding.

I frowned, still reading. "She wasn't running *from* the warden. She *was* a warden."

Daniel balked. "Your mother was the Warden of the West?" He snatched the letter and began to scan the remainder of the contents. "Do you have any idea what a prestigious position that is?"

I plucked the letter from his eager fingertips. "How would I?"

"A warden's job is to track down the most dangerous paranormal criminals in the country and bring them to justice," Daniel explained. "Your mother must have been incredibly powerful to become a warden. They have to train and it's all very secretive, or at least that's how it used to work. Who knows now? To say I'm out of the loop is an understatement."

My hands were shaking. I'd just discovered a crucial piece of my mother's history. Of *my* history.

"Read the next one," Daniel said. "Maybe there's more. I'm sure that's why she entrusted you to the Harts. It would have been very dangerous for a warden to have a child. You would've been an easy mark for revenge seekers. I'm surprised she was allowed to have a child at all."

"And that must've been why it was dangerous for her to

visit me. Someone might have followed her to the Harts." My heart seized as the realization hit me. Maybe someone did. Maybe that was the reason my mother died and, later, my father. Nausea rolled over me. Was I the reason my parents had died so horribly?

I began to read the next letter. "Dearest Geri and Barron, I beg you to bestow much love and kisses upon my darling child. I have dreamed of her as of late, and a prophet I met sees much that is fair and folly in her future. I fervently hope her life is more peaceful than my own, and that her identity remains concealed, as mine often is. Witch, enchantress, sorceress—it makes no difference. They are all me beneath the surface. I play the role my job requires. There is far too much evil in the world, and I shall eradicate such threats one by one for the sake of my child. For the sake of all children. Such is my calling."

Daniel grinned. "Like mother, like daughter."

"I hardly think what I do here is on par with being a Warden of the West," I said. "She sounds like an FBI agent, taking on aliases and catching hardened criminals." I shuddered. "Too scary for me."

"You're braver than you think," Daniel said, echoing the Winnie the Pooh books that I'd once loaned him from the library.

"There's brave and then there's nuts," I replied.

He kissed my cheek. "To be fair, you're a little nuts, too."

"All the best ones are."

"Finish the letter," Daniel urged. He appeared as invested as I felt.

I resumed reading the letter. "The prophet also warned of the reappearance of her father, so please take great care and ward the property to the best of your ability. Protect my precious child. His betrayal still cuts deep and I have no doubt his search for her continues. Despite what he claims, his intentions are not honorable. They never were, of that I am certain."

I paused, drinking in the words. My father betrayed her. Who was he? I scanned the letter again, disappointed that she failed to name him.

"Sounds like your father might have been one of her marks," Daniel said.

"You think she fell in love with a criminal?" I asked.

"Maybe she didn't know he was a criminal at the time," Daniel mused. "She says he betrayed her. If they were both pretending to be other paranormals, it's quite possible."

My heart hammered in my chest. This was more information in one letter than I'd been privy to my whole life.

"I think I need to stop reading now," I said, beginning to feel dizzy. It was too overwhelming and I needed time to digest what I'd learned. "Let's keep this between us so far, okay? I want to get through the rest of the letters before I say anything to anyone."

"Except me," Gareth said.

"I forgot you were even here," I said.

"You told me to stay quiet," he replied.

I arched an eyebrow. "And since when do you do as I tell you?"

He folded his ghostly arms. "Once in a blood moon, it's been known to happen."

"Well, I live with you, so it's kind of hard to avoid sharing personal information. You'd have heard it sooner or later."

"That's because you talk to yourself out loud," Daniel said, grinning.

"All the best people do," I said, echoing my earlier statement.

Daniel chuckled. "Is that so? I had no idea. I'll have to start flying around town, talking to myself." He tackled me onto the sofa, tickling me. "Should I kiss my fiancée? Or should I wait until after we eat? What would she think if I told her how beautiful she looked reading her mother's letters?"

"Ugh," Gareth complained. "I don't need you to share this kind of personal information. This is nauseating."

I didn't notice when he disappeared. I was too preoccupied with staring into Daniel's turquoise eyes. They were my safe place. I could get lost in them and still know with absolute certainty that I would be all right.

"You could say anything to me, Daniel, and I would think I'm the luckiest paranormal on the whole planet."

"No," he said, kissing me deeply. "That's me, hands down."

CHAPTER 15

I WAS JUST ABOUT to open Sigmund's door to drive to the office when someone grabbed me from behind. Before I could yell, my mouth was sealed shut by some kind of spell. I struggled to part my lips but to no avail. As I craned my neck to catch a glimpse of my assailant, a blindfold appeared over my eyes and I felt myself lift into the air. I floated away from Sigmund, pulled by an invisible force.

Although I tried not to panic, my brain betrayed me. Fear flooded my mind and I could barely finish a coherent thought. I attempted to summon my magic to remove the blindfold and the silencing spell, but nothing seemed to work. Where was I being taken?

Fifteen stress-inducing minutes later, someone ripped the blindfold from my eyes and I heard a crescendo of voices yell, "Surprise!"

I blinked, thoroughly confused. I recognized one of the rooms in the Spellbound Country Club. More importantly, I recognized the faces in the room. All my female friends were here. The remedial witches, Agnes, Lucy, the harpies, Dr. Hall, Astrid, and Britta. Even the Grey sisters left their cave

147

together for the occasion. The only one missing was Raisa and that was understandable.

"I told you I'd manage to surprise you," Agnes said with a victorious cackle.

"I thought I was being kidnapped," I said, feeling my heartbeat slow to a normal rate. "Did you have to go to such extreme measures?"

"We're sorry, Emma," Begonia said. "We tried to encourage her to surprise you another way." Translation: we couldn't control the crazy witch. Message received.

"That's okay," I said. "I'm fine now, but why aren't we in the care home? I thought you planned to have it there."

"Special dispensation," Agnes said. "I have a hall pass and I'm not afraid to use it."

"And a vow to perform no magic, let's not forget," Lady Weatherby said pointedly. "A rule you already seem to have broken."

Agnes gave her daughter a sly smile. "Whatever do you mean, Jacinda Ruth? I wouldn't dream of breaking a vow."

"This place looks amazing," I said. There were floating candles near the cathedral ceiling that cast a soft glow throughout the room. Even Octavia Minor appeared more youthful bathed in flattering light. Instead of a typical table, there were floating trays full of nibbles that rotated slowly around the room, pausing in front of each guest.

"Bridal showers are sort of new to us," Begonia said. "We tried to take what we've learned from..." She nearly said 'television,' but stopped herself. The magic mirror in the secret lair was still very much on a need-to-know basis. "From you, Emma."

"Well, I can't claim to be an expert," I said, "but color me impressed."

"And presents," Millie said, pointing to the table against

the wall that was laden with gift boxes. "Mine is that really big one with the yellow bow."

I bit back a smile. "Thank you, Millie. I'm sure I'll love it, big or small."

"And there's chocolate cake," Britta added. "Maybe we could start with that."

Astrid slapped her sister's arm. "We don't start with the cake."

"But it's just sitting there, staring at us," Britta complained.

"If the cake is staring at us, I'm concerned about eating it," Astrid said, deadpan.

The multi-tiered cake was adorned with white icing in the shape of angel wings. "That's so sweet," I said.

"I sure hope so, considering all the sugar I added," Lucy said.

"You made the cake?" I gaped at Lucy. "You're the mayor. When did you have time to bake a cake as fancy as this?"

"My assistant helped," Lucy admitted. "And I may have used a little fairy magic."

"There's nothing wrong with magical assistance," Laurel said.

"First, we're going to play games," Agnes said, with a wicked gleam in her eyes.

I groaned. "Not tiddlywinks?"

Agnes waved me off. "Hell, no. I only play that with professionals. We're going to play games suited to the occasion."

An uneasy feeling crept over me. "And where would you have learned such games?"

"We may have offered suggestions," Sophie said. "From, you now, human world stuff you told us."

I sincerely hoped they weren't basing their ideas off

American television shows. Those events rarely reflected reality.

"Before we start on games, you should wear the trash hat we made for you," Britta said, producing an object that looked like something between a garbage can and a garden. With a proud smile, she placed the item on my head and gave the top an extra tap for good measure.

Everyone scrutinized me.

"It looks...nice," Begonia said tentatively.

I didn't have the heart to tell them that these types of hats were usually made during the shower from paper plates and other accessories.

"Thank you," I said, with as much sincerity as I could muster.

"And now for the games." Agnes retrieved a bottle from the table behind her. "Goddess Bounty, anyone?"

I balked. "A drinking game?"

Agnes eyed me. "Why not? It's a party, isn't it?"

I shot a glance at Laurel. "Maybe we can do that game later."

"Spoilsport," Agnes grumbled.

Petra Grey attempted to remove the bottle from Agnes's tight grip. "Here. Hold this for you, I will."

Agnes held firm. "I don't need help from you, Cyclops. I can hold a bottle just fine."

Millie raised her wand and performed a spell that replicated the sound of a buzzer. "One-two-three. All eyes on me."

The room quieted and everyone turned their attention to Millie.

"Our first game is Purse Raid," Millie announced. "I was in charge of this one, so it should exceed expectations."

"As though we had any doubt," Lady Weatherby said.

"I wanted to call it Handbag Hoopla," Agnes grumbled.

"But there was no arguing with that one." She jerked her thumb toward Millie.

I fought the urge to laugh. Leave it to Millie to overpower the senior witch's will.

"Listen up, everybody," Millie said, clapping her hands loudly. "I'm going to read one item at a time from a list. If you have the item in your purse, let us know."

"Handbag," Agnes said loudly, disguised as a cough.

Millie ignored her. "The one who ends up with the most items on the list wins a prize."

Excitement rippled through the guests.

"You mean we can get gifts even though it's not our special event?" Marisol Minor asked. The entire harpy contingency was present and accounted for.

"Only if you win," Millie said. "First item on the list is easy. Lipgloss or lipstick. Either is acceptable."

A majority of the guests raised their lipsticks in the air. Since I was the guest of honor, I opted to watch the game instead of participate. It was far more enjoyable that way.

Britta waved a chapstick. "Does this count?"

"I'm afraid not," Millie said primly.

"But it tastes like strawberries," Britta objected.

Millie observed the Valkyrie coolly. "An item that tastes like strawberries is not on the list."

"Well, maybe it should be," Britta muttered.

"Next item is a wand," Millie said, clearly ready to move on.

"No fair," Phoebe complained. "Only fairies and witches will have wands. You've already narrowed the field."

"There'll be plenty of items and not everyone will have them all," Sophie said. "Don't count yourself out yet."

Phoebe took a begrudging sip of lemon fizz. "I don't taste any alcohol."

"That's because you're already drunk," Octavia shot back.

Several fairies and witches twirled their wands in the air.

"How about a cat treat?" Millie asked.

When all of the witches admitted to cat treats, I cast a suspicious glance at Agnes. "You don't have a cat."

"Not anymore," she said. "But I still carry treats when I go out. Habit." She popped one into her mouth and chewed. "Plus, they're delicious."

"A receipt for a latte from Brew-Ha-Ha," Millie said.

Althea waved hers in the air. "I've got a million of these."

"No doubt," I said with a laugh. "You should probably throw them away."

"They're work expenses," Althea replied. "I need to keep a record. Gareth taught me that."

"Tweezers," Millie called.

Octavia Minor plucked a pair of tweezers from her purse and held them aloft. "For those stubborn chin hairs you discover in the middle of the market."

"You don't even wait until you get home to remove them?" Lady Weatherby asked, aghast.

"Why put off until later what you can do right away?" Octavia mused. "I use the reflective glass on the sunglasses for a closer look."

"I hadn't thought of that," Lucy said.

"That's because you don't have to worry with that flawless skin," Octavio griped. "And you could always just use magic to get rid of yours."

It suddenly occurred to me that I never needed to use a razor again if I didn't want to. There had to be a spell I could use to remove unwanted hair on my legs. What an epiphany!

"This shower is amazing," I declared.

"You're welcome," Agnes said.

Millie snapped her fingers to get everyone's attention. She was loving her role as game show host. "Next item is a figurine."

Surprisingly, more than one guest copped to having a figurine in a purse.

Althea held up a small garden gnome with a bright orange hat. "Amanda gave it to me yesterday and I haven't had a chance to put it in the garden yet."

Begonia held up a pinky-sized figurine of a begonia. "It was one of the first gifts Demetrius gave to me. I carry it around with me all the time now to remind me how lucky I am."

The women reacted with soft cooing sounds. I always suspected Demetrius was a romantic at heart and now I knew for sure.

"Mage Mace," Millie said.

Half the guests pulled out the same small bottle—the magical equivalent of pepper spray.

"Does Enchanted Irritant count?" Calliope Minor asked.

"Sure," Millie replied.

"Who would use such a thing?" Dr. Hall inquired. "If you need a good defense, just magic yourself a set of fangs." She displayed her own and Calliope winced.

"If I was desperate enough, I'd shift into harpy form," Calliope said. "The spray is a deterrent."

Dr. Hall examined her. "Yeah, you ladies are downright scary when you want to be. Good for you!"

"Something borrowed," Millie called. "If you borrowed an item and it's in your purse, you get five points."

Agnes pulled a second bottle of Goddess Bounty from her handbag. "I may have borrowed this from the liquor shop on the way here."

I smacked my head. "You didn't pay for it?"

"How could I?" Agnes asked. "I didn't have any coins on me."

I shook my head. "Agnes, we have to go back today and pay them. Otherwise, I'll end up defending you in court."

"A pair of underpants," Millie yelled.

"That one was my idea," Lucy said, giggling. She'd been so serious lately, learning the mayoral ropes. It was nice to see her having fun.

Phoebe Minor fished a pair of green lace underpants from her handbag and held them up for all to see. "Don't ask," she said. "Or if you do, be prepared to hear things you wish you hadn't."

Octavia's eyes rolled skyward. "Sometimes I wonder how I managed to produce a harpy like you."

"Pure and simple good luck, I guess," Phoebe said.

Althea laughed heartily and pulled a pair of underpants from her own bag. "I took these from Amanda, too. I thought it was a headscarf." The blue and yellow polka dot underpants were similar to the headscarf she'd been wearing for the past week.

"You win a gift card to Glow," Millie said. "Congratulations, Althea."

Althea hurried to the front to collect her prize. "Ooh, honey, I can sure use that, although some of the fairies there are a little nervous around the girls." She patted her head.

"Next game is 'I Never,'" Agnes announced. "The remedial witches are distributing shot glasses. Sophie's going to read the list."

I inclined my head toward Laurel. "She's too young for this."

Agnes waved me off with her elongated fingernails. "Bah! You should've seen what I was up to at her age."

"I'd rather not imagine it," I said.

Sophie raised her voice. "I'm going to name an activity I've never done. Every time I name one you *have* done, you drink."

"Can I drink either way?" Agnes asked.

"I doubt we could do much to stop you," Lady Weatherby said tersely.

"I never had an owl as a familiar," Sophie said.

I looked at the shot glance in my hand. "Oh, I see how this is going to go." I tipped the glass back and Dr. Hall immediately replaced it with another.

"Just like our sessions," the vampire said with a fanged smile.

"I never fell in love with an angel," Sophie said.

Millie raised her hand. "Does a crush count?"

"Sure," Sophie said.

Half the room drank, including me.

"I never discovered I was a sorceress," Sophie said, not bothering to hide her cheeky smile.

"Hardy har," I said, and drank again. Although the liquid burned my throat, the taste wasn't unpleasant.

"I never stood up to Lady Weatherby," Sophie said, and elbowed Millie. "You can drink for this one."

"So can Emma," Millie said.

"That was only when she was turned into a little girl by the youth spell," I objected.

"I don't have that excuse," Agnes said, and sucked down the amber liquid.

I sipped mine, finding it difficult to finish. If I kept going, I'd be too ill to enjoy the delicious-looking cake.

"I never retrieved the horn of a sacred unicorn," Sophie said.

"Okay, but this is the last one," I said. I forced the last shot down and prayed the contents of my stomach obeyed me.

When I burped, everyone applauded.

Lucy fluttered over to me with a stack of presents.

"There are so many," I said in awe. It didn't help that my head was spinning from the shots.

"More residents sent presents than were invited to the

shower," Lucy explained. "We kept it relatively small, but everyone who heard about it wanted to send a token of goodwill."

"You're the unicorn horn hero," Meg said. "That's going to generate *a lot* of goodwill in this town."

"I only hope it helps," I said. The coven was under so much pressure now to break the curse. Even without a deadline, the proverbial ticking clock was hard at work.

"We're working together," Laurel said. "If that doesn't work, then nothing will."

And no one wanted to contemplate the latter part. Before the mood dampened, I swung into action and summoned a large knife.

"Who's ready for cake?"

CHAPTER 16

ROCHESTER SAT AT HIS DESK, eating a mozzarella, tomato, and basil panini. He had a napkin tucked into his shirt collar, a look that was reminiscent of my grandfather when he ate spaghetti. He always tucked a large white napkin into his shirt to avoid stains because he tended to splatter tomato sauce when he sucked up the strands of spaghetti. Although he showed me how to roll spaghetti around my fork, he was firmly in the do-as-I-say-not-as-I-do camp.

"Emma Hart, what a pleasant surprise," the wizard said. "I haven't seen you since the last committee meeting. Speaking of which, I don't seem to have the next one on my calendar. When will we resume talks on the sentencing guidelines?"

"After the wedding," I said, sitting down across from him. "We've hammered through most of the details at this point. I think it's just cleaning up the proposal before we submit it to the council."

Rochester nodded. "I'm looking forward to that day." He finished the last bite of his panini and wiped his mouth with his napkin. "I have to tell you, Emma. You're a real force of nature. I don't think sweeping changes ever would've happened if you hadn't come to town."

My cheeks warmed. "Oh, I don't know about that. I only expedited things, that's all."

"What brings you here today?" he asked. "Do you need to reschedule the trespassing trial?"

"What I'd actually like is to get the charges dropped and cancel the trial," I said. "I've tried to convince the Akers to talk to you, but they're not budging. I think they're worried about setting a precedent—that they don't care who comes on their property."

Rochester crumpled the panini wrapper and tossed it into the bin. "He was spotted on their property on three separate occasions. Technically, we could charge him with three counts of trespassing."

"I know, but he was never put on notice," I said. "The owners didn't say anything because they were afraid. Tomlin says there were no obvious signs of ownership."

"Not everyone needs an oversized 'Keep Out' sign to put trespassers on notice," Rochester said. "You know that as well as I do, Emma."

I sighed. "I know, but I feel sorry for Tomlin. He lost his neighbor. He's trying to pick up the pieces of his life after his girlfriend left him. He's making an effort to make his life better and I feel like we're making it harder."

Rochester smiled. "And it seems unfair to you."

"Of course it does. We should encourage those who want to do better. To be better."

Rochester tapped the pads of his fingers together. "I'll tell you what. If you can show me that there was no reasonable way your client could have known he was on private property, I'll drop the charges."

My heart soared. "Are you serious?"

"As a vampire funeral parade. Consider it an engagement present."

"I don't want you to do it for me," I said. "I want you to do it because it's fair to Tomlin."

"Sure," Rochester replied. "Slap on whatever reason you want."

"Thank you, Rochester. You have no idea what this will mean to Tomlin."

"I hope it means he does better next time. That it makes him a better citizen of Spellbound."

I cracked open a huge smile. "Me, too."

"You should know that Mayor Knightsbridge petitioned to have her sentence reduced," Rochester said. "She wants to end her house arrest early for good behavior."

The hairs on the back of my neck stood on end. "And what was the outcome?"

"Still pending, but I thought you should know."

"I guess it's hard to demonstrate bad behavior when she's under house arrest," I said. "She can't do much damage from there."

"I'm thinking about paying her a visit," Rochester said. "I'd like to gauge her mindset. See if she still holds a grudge against you."

I bristled. "I'm sure she does. I'm responsible for sending her daughter to prison."

"No," Rochester said firmly. "Only Elsa is responsible for Elsa's imprisonment and don't you forget it."

"Do you think she's trying to get out early because she's heard about the wedding?" I asked. What if she wanted to sabotage it?

"I wouldn't put anything past her at this point," Rochester said. "But, rest assured, no one's taking anything she says at face value. She broke faith with all of us and we won't soon forget it."

"Will you let me know how your visit goes?" I asked.

"Absolutely. Now on to other matters," Rochester said. "Tell me how the wedding plans are coming along."

"Everything's good," I said. "I thought it would be more stressful, but I have so much help. It makes all the difference."

"Sharing the load always makes a difference," Rochester agreed. "No one paranormal should bear all the weight, even for a happy occasion like a wedding."

"The same idea applies to magic, too," I said. I told him how I'd been struggling on my own to retrieve my mother's letters using the manifestation spell. It was only when I harnessed the power of the remedial witches as well that I was able to complete the task successfully.

"I'm happy for you," Rochester said. "It must be an incredible feeling to hold a letter that your biological mother wrote."

"The horrible part is that I've been so busy, I haven't been able to finish reading them."

"You should definitely make time," Rochester said. "You've been waiting for this moment."

"Dr. Hall thinks part of it is fear. That I'm afraid I might read something I don't want to know, so I'm dragging this whole thing out."

Rochester gave me a patient smile. "It's a reasonable assumption, but you're strong, Emma. You'll dig deep and get through it, no matter what the letters say."

"Thank you, Rochester," I said. "I appreciate the support."

"You've been so supportive of everyone here," he replied. "The least we can do is support you in your time of need."

I wanted to hug the kindly wizard. "You're coming to the wedding, right? I haven't done the invitations yet, but I promise you're on the list."

He placed a warm hand on my shoulder. "Wouldn't miss it for the world."

Do we have to do this? Sedgwick complained.

You don't have to, but I do, I said. I shivered as the sun disappeared behind the canopy of trees. Up ahead, the bone-yard cottage set my teeth on edge. No matter how many times I visited Raisa, the feelings never subsided.

How about I wait out here? Sedgwick asked.

She keeps a jar of mice for you, I said. *Now that's a good hostess.*

Plenty of rodents out here in the forest, Sedgwick said. *Besides, I prefer the thrill of the chase.*

Really? And here I always thought you were lazy.

Sedgwick flew off without another word and I banged my fist on the door of the small cottage. It creaked open and I stepped inside.

"Have you ever considered redecorating?" I asked.

Raisa stood at a table, mixing herbs into a bowl. "Why bother? No one visits me anyway."

I removed my cloak and set it on the back of a nearby chair. "I'm no one? Thanks a lot."

She snapped her iron teeth, a reminder that her ghostly form still had one foot (or mouth) in the land of the living. "Sit down, dearie. Have a bowl of my special soup."

I glanced at the bubbling cauldron and the smell wafted over to me. I wasn't sure what made it special, other than the fact that a scary ghost witch was preparing it.

"You're far more advanced than Gareth," I said. "He barely manages not to fall through walls."

"I have far more experience," Raisa said. "And my lingering spirit is of a different sort."

I scrutinized her. "How so? Spirits are spirits, aren't they?"

Raisa's toothpick legs carried her to the cauldron. "That's

like saying witches are witches. Of course they're not all the same. Ghosts—spirits—they have their differences."

"I see your point," I said. "Listen, I came to apologize about you not being invited to the bridal shower. It wasn't a deliberate snub. My friends knew you wouldn't be able to come to the country club."

Raisa stirred the contents of the cauldron. "And they were too frightened to deliver the invitation as well, I reckon."

"Let's face it. Your place isn't exactly homey." I pointed behind me. "That skull above the door could stand to go. Make the cottage more inviting to visitors."

"Perhaps I should add a swipe of lipgloss to it and mascara around the empty eye sockets," Raisa suggested. "Would that do?"

"Congratulations. You've managed to make it creepier. You have a true talent, Raisa."

She peered at me from her place at the cauldron, her face expressionless. "You speak to me like no one else ever dared to."

A chill crept up my spine. "You're not going to toss me into that cauldron as punishment, are you?"

Raisa's laugh was low and—dare I say it—affectionate. "You have warmed to me, haven't you, dearie?"

"Are you suffering from self-esteem issues all of the sudden?" I asked. Raisa had never been particularly well-liked in the Spellbound community. That was part of the reason she lived alone in the woods where no one had even been aware of her death.

Raisa cackled, sounding more like herself. "Hardly. I'll leave those pathetic types of emotions to the living." She scooped out soup with the ladle and poured it into a bowl. "So tell me, dearie, how was this event called a bridal shower?"

"A lot of fun, actually," I said, accepting the bowl. "You

were missed." I sat at the table where a spoon awaited me. "You knew I was coming to see you, huh?"

"Always," Raisa replied. She joined me at the table with her own bowl.

"You first," I said good-naturedly.

"All this time and you still lack trust," she said, although I could tell she wasn't truly offended.

"The first time I came here, you fed me a potion that could've killed me," I reminded her. "Pardon me for being cautious."

"Need I remind you that I'm already dead," Raisa said. "I can suck down the entire cauldron and haunt this cottage for years to come."

I tapped my spoon absently on the table. "Fair point. Now I'm losing my appetite."

"Eat, my dear girl," Raisa insisted. "You need your strength. Dark days lie ahead."

I froze. "What did you say?"

Raisa met my gaze. "It's an expression, dearie. Surely you can decipher its meaning."

I opted to stay silent about my mother's letters. "We're talking about my bridal shower. How do dark days figure into it?"

Raisa flashed a Mona Lisa smile, and I caught a glimpse of her iron teeth that sent a ripple of fear through me. I was pretty sure people admiring the portrait of Mona Lisa in the Louvre didn't have that experience.

"How goes the coven efforts to break the curse?" she asked.

"You're the know-it-all, Miss Dark Days," I said. "You tell me." I swallowed my first spoonful of soup. It tasted like a mixture of chicken broth, spices, and a pinch of something sweet. I desperately hoped there were no snails or puppy dog tails.

Raisa picked up her bowl and drained the soup from it in one impressive gulp. "You're very close, my dear. I feel it in my bones." She glanced around the cottage. "All my bones."

"What will happen to you if we break the curse?" I asked, thinking of Gareth.

"My body is buried here and here I shall remain," Raisa said.

"You won't move on to...anywhere else?" I queried. Heaven, hell, Valhalla, the underworld.

"No, no," she replied. "I am destined to haunt these grounds forevermore. My ghostly prison. Such is my fate."

I swallowed another mouthful of soup. "Do you ever get lonely?"

Raisa cackled again, although the sound was softer this time. "A horrible witch like me doesn't get lonely, Emma. We have earned our solitude."

That seemed an odd thing to say. "That's how Daniel used to feel. That he deserved to be alone without love. It wasn't true, not for him and not for you."

Raisa's bony fingers reached for mine. "Like it or not, you will change us all, dear girl. So pure of heart you still are."

"I thought that was a good thing," I said.

"Oh, make no mistake. It is. Not everyone likes change, however. Many fear it with irrational gusto. We tend to be creatures of comfort, of safety. When someone threatens that existence, we often react negatively."

"Sounds like what Demetrius said." And he wasn't wrong, except we'd been discussing my mother's letters at the time, not the curse. "Are you saying we shouldn't break the curse? That we should leave it be because everyone's used to it?"

"Not at all," Raisa replied. "I only want you to be prepared for the consequences."

"As in 'be careful what you wish for'?" I asked. My stomach felt warm and full.

"Everyone should heed that advice," Raisa said. "Should the coven succeed, there will be sweeping changes in Spellbound, mark my words."

"Because of paranormals choosing to leave?"

"And those choosing to arrive," Raisa said. "The entire character of the town is at risk."

"At risk makes it sound like a bad thing," I said. "Maybe there'll be an influx of wonderful paranormals who can't wait to experience life in Spellbound." I tilted my head. "You were well traveled before you came here. Any chance you were familiar with the term 'Warden of the West?'"

Her eyes grew sharp and focused. "Of course. Enforcer of the East. Warden of the West. Keeper of the North. Sentinel of the South."

"Daniel knew them, too," I said.

"Where have you heard these terms?" Raisa asked. "You weren't familiar with the paranormal world before you came here, as I recall."

"There's a mention of a warden in my mother's letters," I said. "I manifested a packet of her letters from the human world and have been reading through them."

Raisa clucked her tongue. "Your powers are remarkable. And why does your mother discuss such matters? Was she a fugitive of some kind? That wouldn't surprise me. The sorceresses I knew were always in trouble. Too much beauty and power spoils the package."

I finished the last drop of soup. "She wasn't a fugitive. She chased the fugitives. Apparently, she was one of the Wardens of the West."

Raisa fell silent for a beat. "Such a dangerous job, even for a talented sorceress."

"Did you ever meet a warden?" I asked. "Maybe you met my mother once upon a time."

Her sharp features melted into a faraway expression.

"Not the Warden of the West, no. I met the Enforcer of the East once—the European branch--when I was younger and very foolish. He was a genie. Extremely powerful and even brutal when the job required it. I was glad to leave an ocean between us when I came to this country."

"I guess brutal is sometimes a necessity when your job is to apprehend dangerous criminals," I said.

"I suppose." She gave me a quizzical look. "But not for you."

"What's not for me?"

"You would no more be brutal than a fish would walk on land. Though you have much power, your sense of compassion far outweighs it."

"That's nice of you to say," I said. "On the other hand, I don't run after scary criminals who might kill me. Maybe I'd behave differently then. I mean, I threw Mumford across a room with a spell when he attacked me. I'm not above hurting someone else to protect myself."

Raisa pressed her thin lips together. "Self-defense is a very different matter, dearie."

"What was in the soup?" I asked. "And don't say 'nothing' because I know better. I can always taste when you're up to something."

Raisa's pale brow lifted. "You knew and yet you ate it anyway? Why?"

I shrugged. "Because whatever it is, I trust you."

Raisa stood silently for a moment, contemplating her answer. "It was a potion designed to extract information."

That must have been why I revealed the information about my mother, even though I'd originally decided not to mention it.

"You wanted to know about the progress in breaking the curse," I said. "But I would've told you about that anyway."

"I wasn't sure, dearie."

"What's the difference?" I asked. "If you can't leave anyway, why does it matter to you?"

"If the floodgates open, I want to be prepared," she said. "As I said, dark days lie ahead."

I set aside my spoon. "Prepared for what?"

Raisa lifted a bony finger. "Our doom."

CHAPTER 17

THE TIKI BAR was just as swanky and cool as the last time I visited for Markos's opening night party. Since it was off-hours, there were only a handful of customers. I spotted Markos deep in conversation with one of his bartenders over at the Polynesian-style bar. With his seven-foot minotaur frame and giant horns, he was hard to miss. I was surprised to see Beatrice by his side. For an office manager, she seemed to spend a lot of time out of the office and glued to the minotaur. Even though I was wary of the witch, the fact that she appreciated Markos in his true form as much as in his human form spoke volumes to me.

"Emma," Markos exclaimed when he saw me. "I'm so glad you're here."

"I'm sorry Daniel couldn't make it," I said. "He had to help with an emergency at the Spellbound Care Home. There was an issue with the roof. His wings come in handy every once in a while over there."

"Maybe I should go look at the building this week," Markos said. "I bet they could use a little renovation to spruce things up."

"That's a wonderful idea," I said. "I don't think the building has been updated in quite some time. With your talent, I'm sure you could come up with something amazing." And the paranormals who lived there deserved amazing.

Markos grinned. "Beatrice and I had just been discussing charitable projects for the coming year. The care home would be a worthwhile project, for sure."

That was one of the things I loved about Markos. As successful as he was, he was constantly thinking of ways to pay it forward. He didn't just collect his gold coins and move on. Instead, he tried to find ways to improve existing structures, as well as create new ones.

"Would you like a drink?" Beatrice asked.

I hesitated. I wasn't sure that I trusted Beatrice enough to get me a drink. With her track record, she'd probably put a diarrhea spell on the liquid before passing it to me.

"No, thank you," I said. "I'm only here to check out the menu for the reception." Although revisiting the space now, I was forced to acknowledge the venue was too small for our guests. I didn't want to disappoint Markos, though.

"Brad has a copy of the drinks menu," Markos said. "We have several packages to choose from."

I took the list of packages and studied it. The offerings were much more interesting than those offered by the country club, not that I was surprised. Markos had a penchant for creativity, even in the food and beverage industry.

"Beatrice, would you do me a favor and grab the dessert packages from inside?" Markos asked. "I left the papers on my desk."

Once Beatrice slid off the stool and retreated indoors, Markos turned his enormous minotaur face back to me. "I know I'm probably spitting in the wind here, but is there any chance you might change your mind?"

"Change my mind?" I asked. "You mean about where to have the reception?"

His eyes bored into mine. "Not where to have it, but whether to have it at all."

I placed my hand on his bulging arm. "Markos, you know I care for you, but I love Daniel wholly and completely. There's no one else in the world for me. Besides, if you stopped to really think about it, you'd realize you're already over me. You just haven't admitted it to yourself yet."

His large forehead furrowed. "I'm not sure what you mean."

I smiled. "I mean a pretty witch by the name of Beatrice. You can't possibly tell me that you don't have feelings for her. The two of you already look like an old married couple, and I mean that in the best possible way."

Markos rubbed one of his horns thoughtfully. "Really? I've been under the impression that we have a nice compatible employer–employee relationship. You think it's more than that?"

I rolled my eyes. Some men were so clueless. "I've seen the way she looks at you, Markos. Trust me, that is not the way an employee typically looks at her boss. But what I've noticed even more is the way *you* look at *her*. I think maybe your brain just hasn't caught up to your heart."

Markos snorted. "It wouldn't surprise me." He appeared thoughtful for a moment. "She's never once cringed at the sight of my natural form. I know for a fact there were other employees at my firm that needed to get used to me walking around in full-blown minotaur mode. But Beatrice has only ever showed respect and affection."

"Sounds like an ideal partner to me," I said.

"I'm sorry it took so long," Beatrice's voice interjected. "It was hidden under a pile of order forms."

Markos chuckled. "Looks like I might need an office manager in *all* my offices."

Beatrice handed me the packages menu. As with the drinks menu, Markos's creativity was on full display. Each dessert was more sumptuous than the last one.

"My only concern is that my place is too small for your guest list," Markos said. "Between you and Daniel, I would think you'd end up inviting most of the town."

"To be honest, that's my concern, too," I said, relieved that he'd mentioned it. "Then again, I don't think there's anywhere big enough to accommodate all the paranormals we want to include." Even the country club had a maximum limit.

"I completely understand if you need to go in another direction," Markos said. "I'd just really like to be involved somehow as more than a guest. You've done so much for me, Emma. I only want to return the favor."

"Your friendship has been more than enough," I said. "The paranormals in this town have changed my life." An idea took shape as I glanced around the Tiki Bar. "What if we *did* want to invite the whole town?" There truly wasn't any place large enough to hold everyone.

"What are you thinking?" Markos asked. "The grounds of the Mayor's Mansion?"

"No. What if we held multiple receptions at the same time? That way we could include everyone and also get to patronize our favorite places."

Markos stared at me. "I know Daniel is well off, but will he want to spend so much money on receptions he won't even attend?"

"I think we will attend, though," I said. "Let's not forget the guy has wings. He can fly us from one reception to another throughout the evening, so we get the chance to spend time with everyone. And even those who don't know us will still get to have a great night."

"You'll effectively shut down the whole town," Markos said. "The council will probably make you apply for a special permit."

"Fine with me," I said. "This is the perfect opportunity for Daniel and I to thank everyone for making Spellbound the special place that it is. A town is nothing without the people...or paranormals who inhabit it."

The more I thought about it, the more I warmed to the idea. A huge party that included everyone in town. It would be unprecedented. Shifters, fairies, pixies, dwarfs, and witches. Every paranormal under the moon.

"There's something I need to tell you both," Beatrice blurted.

"You don't like the reception idea?" I asked. It wasn't a perfect plan, of course. We'd need to split up the guests and they'd be scattered across town.

Beatrice shook her dark head. "Emma, I've been wrong about you and I want to come clean." She hesitated, her gaze shifting to Markos. Whatever she was about to say seemed to make her very nervous.

Markos sensed her discomfort. "What's wrong, Beatrice?"

The witch turned back to me with a pinched expression. "I was the one who put you in the waking nightmare in Dr. Hall's office." She lowered her head. "I'm also the one who poisoned your plant."

I'd suspected the waking nightmare. The plant, however, took me by surprise. "The one in my office? You broke in and poisoned my plant?" It wasn't me she had to worry about—it was Althea's wrath. The Gorgon had been very attached to that plant.

Tears spilled down Beatrice's alabaster cheeks. "I was so jealous of you that I couldn't think straight. Every time I was with Markos, he mentioned your name. It didn't matter that you were with Daniel, I still could tell he had feelings for you and that I would never stand a chance." She fished a tissue out of her pocket and blew her nose. "I'm really sorry. Those were terrible things to do and it's not who I am. You're a good paranormal, Emma, and I can see why he would fall for you. You do all of these selfless tasks for others, and so does Markos. All I've been concerned with is myself." She looked up at the minotaur. "I don't deserve you, Markos. You deserve someone like Emma."

I wasn't sure what to say. I didn't want to speak for Markos, but given our conversation a few minutes ago, I knew Beatrice was wrong about his feelings.

Markos cupped her chin in his oversized paw. "It took a lot of courage for you to confess to both of us like this. To me, that shows your true character."

She wiped her cheeks with another tissue. "I'm so happy to hear that, but it's really Emma I've wronged."

My chest tightened as I watched the witch blow her nose again. How could I not forgive someone with so much love in her heart, she was willing to risk losing Markos by telling the truth?

"I forgive you, Beatrice," I said. "We all make mistakes. It's how we handle them that matters. And I think you and Markos have more in common than you might believe."

Beatrice scrunched her nose. "We do?"

"You're a good witch, Beatrice," Markos said. "And smart, beautiful, incredibly organized…"

I laughed. "I don't think her organizational skills are what made you fall in love with her."

"Markos…He loves me?" She didn't dare meet his gaze for fear of seeing the wrong answer in his eyes.

He bent down and kissed her wet cheek. "Markos does. And he's sorry he didn't see it sooner."

Beatrice smiled through her tears. "Can Markos stop talking about himself in the third person? It's making Beatrice question her choices."

When they laughed, the sound echoed in the night air. I couldn't have been more thrilled for them.

"I'd like to have Nameless Faces play for the reception here," I said, my mind racing. If we held the reception at multiple venues, we could have Look Mom, No Wings play at Moonshine, too. It would be an incredible night for the whole town. "And we'll take the two largest packages for drinks and dessert."

"How will you divide up the guests?" Markos asked. "I imagine the shifters will want to be together."

I shook my head. "Nope. Everyone is getting mixed up. This is going to be like high school." I thought of the wide range of paranormals exiting the high school when I went to see Sean. A melting pot. A potpourri. A cornucopia. Whatever it was, it was beautiful and that was exactly what I wanted for our wedding day.

"Congratulations, Emma," Markos said. "I have a feeling your wedding is going to be one for the Spellbound history books."

I did, too. I only hoped it was for the right reasons.

CHAPTER 18

Now that Rochester had given me a chance to get the charges against Tomlin dropped, I wasted no time getting out to the Akers' land. I was about to start a brand new chapter in my life and I wanted the same for the werelynx.

I drove Sigmund back to the Akers' property to gather evidence to present to the wizard prosecutor. Sedgwick flew above the car, never one to miss an opportunity to hunt.

You drive like an old, blind woman, he said.

And you complain like one, I countered.

Maybe you can have your wedding reception out here, Sedgwick suggested. *This place is big enough to fit everyone in town.*

For some reason, I doubt the Akers would agree to it. They seem to dislike trespassers.

When are you going to talk to Daniel about the multiple receptions? the owl asked.

When I have time, I huffed. *As you can see, I've been a little busy.*

I think you're stalling.

I have complete confidence Daniel will love the idea, I said.

Not to take the spotlight off you, Bridezilla, but I don't see any signs of a boundary, Sedgwick said. *Not from this vantage point.*

Last I checked, a werelynx lacked the ability to fly, I said. *I'll check things out from the ground, thanks.*

I'll shout if I see any dung piles, Your Highness, the owl said. *Wouldn't want you to ruin a perfectly good pair of shoes.*

I would appreciate that. I parked the car on the side of the road and stopped to study the perimeter of the field. Nothing obvious here. I trudged across the land, scanning for any sign of ownership. Tomlin was right. I could see the Akers' house in the distance, but it was unclear they owned this patch of property.

I surveyed the ground, careful to avoid stepping on poop or roots. There were loads of wild vegetables growing here. It was obvious why Tomlin thought this was a good place to forage. The vegetables weren't in neat rows, nor did they appear to be cared for by anyone except Mother Nature.

Poop alert, two o'clock, Sedgwick said.

I glanced at the ground slightly to my right. *I don't see any.*

Not yet, he said. *Incoming!*

I hopped to the left as Sedgwick dropped a bomb. "Hey! There's a whole field here. No need to cut it so close."

Sedgwick chuckled. *Sorry. When you've got to go, you've got to go.*

I turned my attention back to the field, determined to ignore my cheeky familiar. *All these vegetables are making me hungry. Now I want to go home and make a stew.*

Sedgwick flew down to investigate. *Throw a few mice in and I'm all over it.*

I wrinkled my nose. "No, thank you. Now I've lost my appetite."

He settled on a nearby stump. *I won't tell if you want to take anything away as, you know, evidence.*

"You won't tell because no one else can hear you," I said.

"But I have no interest in stealing from the Akers. They've felt traumatized enough."

Aren't you technically trespassing? Sedgwick asked.

"I have permission to investigate the area," I said. At least I hoped so. I probably should have gotten that in writing. I didn't want to end up defending myself in court.

I inspected the variety of plants and vegetables. "I wonder why the Akers don't use these for food. I see rosemary, carrots, and parsnip…" An image flashed in my mind of the plants in Janis Goodfellow's magical greenhouse.

What's wrong? Sedgwick asked. *You've got that weird look on your face like you know your pants are too tight, but you want to justify why you should still wear them.*

"First of all, there's no expression that says all that," I said. "Second of all, I think I may be wrong."

You? Wrong? Sedgwick asked with mock horror. *Now that's something I'd like to get in writing.*

I crouched down to inspect the parsnip. "I don't think this is a vegetable, Sedgwick. I think it's hemlock."

Hemlock does grow in the wild, Sedgwick said.

"I know," I said. "I learned all about it from Janis. I'd like to take some to her to confirm my findings."

Don't touch it, Sedgwick warned. *Even skin contact can have a negative effect on you.*

"Aw, I'm so touched that you care," I replied.

I don't want you to look like a circus freak on your wedding day and scare your guests. He paused. *On second thought, go on and touch it.*

"I need to find something to dig it up with," I said. I ended up using a stick to dig the root out of the ground and then wrapped it in a few burdock leaves to carry it.

A noise across the field drew my attention. I rose to my feet to look around. "Oh no. I hope it's not the Akers," I said.

It's probably an animal, Sedgwick said. *I saw quite a few from the air. Even a skunk.*

"Could you make yourself useful and scope out the area?" I asked. "If it's the Akers, I don't want them to attack me."

Sedgwick took to the skies and flew in a long circle as I made my way back to the car.

Any sign? I asked.

No signs of land ownership. No signs of the Akers. Basically, no signs.

I got into my car and drove straight to Janis Goodfellow's. There was no time to waste. If Janis confirmed that the plant was hemlock rather than parsnip, I'd have my answer.

Well, the good news is that Rochester will probably drop the charges against your client, Sedgwick said.

Yes, but the bad news is that if what I'm thinking is right, I said, *trespassing is going to be the least of poor Tomlin's concerns.*

The first thing I noticed when I stepped into my office was the blossoming plant on my windowsill. The second thing I noticed was the large vat located behind my chair. Given its size and shiny silver coating, I probably should've noticed it first.

I tapped on Althea's adjoining door. "I see you decided to make some improvements to my office."

The door jerked open and Althea appeared in the doorway. "Am I supposed to know what you're talking about?"

I gestured toward the two new additions. Her expression brightened. "It's not even my birthday. What's the occasion?" She sauntered into the room and went to inspect the plant. "She's a beauty. We'll take good care of you, won't we?"

"I thought you brought these," I said.

"No, Miss Boss," she said. "I haven't been in here all day. I was waiting for you to roll out of bed."

I laughed. "You know I don't stay in bed all day, right? I do other things before I come here." Sorceress training, academy classes, wedding planning, therapy…the list was endless.

"Sure. Other things like sleep." Althea stroked the leaves of the plant. "This one's absolutely gorgeous. Oh, look. There's a note." She snatched it from where it was nestled near the soil and began to read. "It's addressed to both of us." Her snakes hissed as she continued to read. "Beatrice murdered our plant? Did you know that?"

"Not for very long," I admitted. "I was waiting to see if she would tell you herself. I guess this is her way of making amends."

Althea inclined her head toward the vat of what I had no doubt was moonshine. "She's doing a pretty good job, I'll say that much. You're cool with her now?"

I told Althea about our conversation at the Tiki Bar. "I worried at first that she was going to turn into another Elsa, but she's so much better than that." Anyone who was brave enough to confess to Althea and try to make things right was okay in my book.

"She was even smart enough to store the vat in your office," Althea said. "That shows good judgment."

"I'm glad you think so, because you're going to be sitting next to her at the reception."

Althea seemed surprised. "I assumed I'd be sitting with Amanda and Miranda. Everyone always lumps us Gorgons together."

"We're mixing things up this time, Althea," I said. "Whatever happens, it's going to be a night to remember."

Althea gave me a pointed look. "Be careful what you wish for, Emma."

"Don't worry," I said. "Everything's under control."

"Good, because I've got a nail appointment. Seeing your cuticles last week reminded me I'm long past due."

Heat warmed my cheeks. "Maybe you should make me an appointment while you're there."

"I insist on it."

Twenty minutes later, I sat at my desk, pretending to review Tomlin's file. It was difficult to focus on the words. My mind kept drifting to the complexities of life and the choices we make. Sometimes even when we try to be the best versions of ourselves, we fall short. At least changes were coming to the sentencing guidelines. That made me feel a little bit better about what was about to happen, but I took no pleasure in it.

The office door opened and Tomlin popped his head inside. "Are you ready for me?"

I waved him in. "Right on time."

"I come bearing gifts," he said, and lifted a coffee cup in each hand. "Every time I've been to see you, your assistant has given you a latte. I figured I'd save her the trouble this time."

My heart sank. Tomlin was a good paranormal. He didn't deserve this unfortunate turn of events. "Thank you so much," I said, accepting the latte. I took a sip and sighed contentedly. "I don't know what I'd do without Brew-Ha-Ha."

Tomlin sat in the chair across from me and grinned. "You'd start going to Perky's."

"I guess that's true, but it wouldn't be the same. Not for me."

Tomlin sipped from his own cup. "So you said you had information to share. Have they dismissed the trespassing charges against me?"

"Unfortunately not," I said. "But I wouldn't worry about that right now because you're going to have bigger dragons to slay."

Tomlin's eyes widened. "Bigger dragons? What does that mean?"

I took another sip of my latte and the liquid warmed my insides, despite the slightly bitter taste. "Did you get the extra shot of confidence?"

"No, is that what you normally have? I added a shot of luck," he replied.

My brow creased. "A shot of luck? I didn't even know they offered that." They should promote it to the casino crowd.

Tomlin remove the lid from his cup and blew off the steam. "So tell me about the bigger dragon. Sounds serious."

"It is. I went to the Akers' property again to have another look at the borders."

"And?" he prompted.

"I noticed something." I paused. My stomach began to feel funny. I was probably nervous about what I was about to say. "I found wild hemlock growing there."

"I didn't realize hemlock grew naturally here," Tomlin said.

"It's rare," I said. "But there are a few places in town and, apparently, you discovered one of them. The Akers weren't even aware because they neglect that space." I met his gaze. "You didn't realize when you dug it up because it looks just like parsnip."

Tomlin appeared stunned. "Hemlock looks like parsnip? How would I know that? I'm not a wizard."

"You wouldn't know that," I said reassuringly. "To the untrained eye, it looks like a root vegetable. Anyone could have made that mistake, Tomlin."

Tomlin's lips formed a regretful line. "Seamus and I had made up. The stew was a peace offering, like I told you. I didn't realize there was anything wrong. Even after I came back to the house and saw him losing muscle control, I didn't know why."

"And remind me why you left? You didn't want to try your own stew?"

"No, no. I'd planned for us to eat the stew together, but I forgot the oregano that I wanted to sprinkle on top. It was the piece de resistance, as Geena used to say. I didn't want to leave it out, so I ran home for it."

"But then you never ate the stew," I said.

"How could I? I was too busy watching Seamus die," he said, his voice raw with emotion. "I didn't want to touch the stew after that. I even threw out the leftovers. I still consider myself lucky that I didn't eat it. When the autopsy report came back, I knew I'd dodged a silver bullet." He stopped talking and his face reddened.

I studied him. "How would the autopsy report have tipped you off that it was your stew? You said you didn't know anything about wild hemlock."

Tomlin sipped his latte. "Okay, fine. Geena had warned me about it one time when she persuaded me to go foraging with her. I'd forgotten her little sermon until I heard the autopsy results, then it all came rushing back to me and I realized what had happened. So now you know the truth. Happy?"

"Of course I'm not happy," I said, my frustration evident. "Why didn't you turn yourself in? You even tried to direct me to Sean!"

"I honestly wasn't trying to mislead you there," Tomlin replied. "I wasn't thinking about it when I mentioned his visit. I convinced myself I'd done nothing wrong. It's amazing the lies we tell ourselves to get through the day."

"And I guess you told us about Seamus's fight with Maxwell before you knew it was your stew."

"That's right," he said. "I'm not a complete monster."

He could've fooled me. In fact, it seemed that he had. At

that moment, the coffee cup slipped from my hand. My fingers seemed to be disconnected from my body.

"Tomlin," I choked. "Did you put hemlock in my latte?"

Tomlin gave me a rueful smile. "I told you I added a shot of luck. I just neglected to mention the luck was for me."

I gaped at him. "Why?" My other hand began to feel numb.

"I saw you at the Akers' property that day," he admitted. "I was trying to do the same as you. Figure out whether there was a clear boundary for the trespassing case so I could help get it dismissed. I didn't want to avoid a murder charge only to be sent away for a trespassing charge. I was in my lynx form. That's why you didn't see me. We're very stealthy creatures when we need to be."

My throat became dry. "How could you tell I knew what had happened?"

"Your expression," he said. "You were shocked when you discovered what looked like parsnip. I realized then that you'd figured it out. I'd considered digging up the whole field of them before then, but it was impossible with those nosy wereferrets around."

"I wasn't even sure whether you knew what you'd done," I said. "I thought maybe it would come as a surprise to you now." Clearly not. The realization was both disappointing and horrifying. I wanted Tomlin to be better than this. I wanted everyone to be better than this. "So now you've gone and poisoned me, too?"

"I'm starting to turn my life around and I can't let you ruin it. It isn't fair."

My pulse began to slow. "And this is fair to me how? I only want to help you."

"But you'll have to turn me in," Tomlin argued. "You'd never get away with ignoring the evidence."

My body weakened. "And you'll never get away with this."

"Sure I will. I checked first that Althea wasn't here before giving it to you," he said. He took my cup and wiped the outside of it with a cloth from his pocket. "Anyone could have poisoned your latte. You have powerful enemies, you know. Mayor Knightsbridge is already under house arrest. It wouldn't be difficult to pin this on her."

My chest tightened. "You forgot one thing."

"What's that?"

"After I confirmed it was hemlock with Janis Goodfellow, I told Astrid what I knew," I said. "I asked her to meet me here after I got your side of the story. I knew what I had to do, as difficult as it was. It shouldn't be long now." Too late for me, but not too late to catch the killer.

"No, it shouldn't." Tomlin shot out of the chair like a rocket.

As weak as I felt, I mustered the strength to conjure a quick spell. "As gentle as a morning breeze/make this lying werelynx freeze."

The basic spell was all I could manage. I slouched in the chair, too incapacitated to move. The door flew open and Astrid appeared. She took one look in the room and knew there was a problem. She bypassed the frozen werelynx and rushed to my side.

"Emma," she said, and I heard the note of urgency in her voice. "What's wrong? Is it hemlock?"

My head lolled to the side. "I feel it now." The words came slowly, but they came.

"There's no antidote for hemlock, right?" she said. Her expression was frantic. I'd never seen the Valkyrie look scared before. "I need to get the healer here, but I don't want to leave you."

The adjoining door opened and I caught sight of Althea's concerned face as my eyes began to flutter.

"What in Hades' name?" the Gorgon said. Her snakes

184

hissed wildly. "I leave for one lousy nail appointment and this is what I come back to?"

The scene must have looked insane to her with a frozen werelynx and the sheriff hovering over me as I slumped in the chair.

"Tomlin has poisoned Emma with hemlock," Astrid said. "I need you to go for the healer. If he doesn't get here soon, she won't make it."

Althea came to stand beside us. "There's nothing a druid can do for this, Sheriff Astrid."

The Valkyrie grimaced. "What are you saying? There's nothing we can do? She's still alive. We have a chance."

Althea began to unwrap her headscarf. "I said there's nothing the druid can do. I didn't say there was nothing *I* could do. Close your eyes, Sheriff."

Althea gently closed my eyes with her index finger.

"You're going to put her out of her misery before the hemlock can take effect?" Astrid queried.

"Don't be ridiculous. I'm a Gorgon, girl," she said, and I heard the snap of her fingers. "My snakes have abilities that most paranormals aren't even aware of."

"Some kind of healing venom?" Astrid asked.

"No, but wouldn't that be nice? What my snakes do have are two hollow fangs each where they can store their venom if they feel the need," Althea explained.

"What good will venom do?"

"Not their venom, Sheriff. Their hollow fangs. Do you follow?"

"You're going to have the snakes suck the poison from her blood and store it in their hollow fangs?" Astrid sounded incredulous.

"Need I remind you," Althea said, "these are no ordinary snakes."

"Will they hurt her?" Astrid's voice was shaking.

"Not as much as dying will," Althea said.

I didn't like the sound of that. I had a wedding aisle to march down in a matter of weeks. Whatever she was proposing, I wanted her to hurry up and do it.

Astrid hesitated. "Go on then. Do it now."

I felt Althea kneel beside me as she took my bare arm in her hands. My arms were so numb, I didn't feel any pain when their fangs pierced my flesh. I don't know how many snakes were feeding on me, but I hoped there were enough to get the job done. I tried to stay conscious, but when darkness finally came, I was too weak to fight it.

CHAPTER 19

WHEN I AWOKE, my arm felt like I'd donated blood a hundred times over. I raised my head to look for Astrid and Althea, and quickly realized I was no longer in my office. This was my bed in my own home. When did that happen?

Gareth's grumpy face appeared next to mine. "If you want to die so badly, all you need to do is ask. I have plenty of resources at my disposal."

I broke into a smile. "I'm not Socrates," I said. "I didn't know I was sucking down a hemlock latte."

"I'll let Halo Boy know you're awake," he said. "He's been driving me to distraction with his constant pacing."

"How will you manage that?" I asked. "Daniel can't hear you."

Gareth wiggled his eyebrows. "I'll have Magpie do the dirty work."

I winced at the thought of the hellbeast attempting to herd Daniel upstairs. "Keep him in check, please. I don't need any more drama today."

Welcome back, Sleeping Beauty, Sedgwick said from his perch.

As I sat up and tried to smooth my hair, my fingers got caught in the knots. "Ouch. I need a brush."

Whoa. Let's revise my statement to simply 'welcome back.'

Before I had a chance to reply, Daniel bolted through the doorway. The angel practically smothered me with relieved kisses.

"You can breathe now. I'm okay," I reassured him.

His lips brushed against mine. "I didn't save you from drowning in Swan Lake so that you could die from hemlock poisoning."

"I do believe *I'm* the one who saved *you* at Swan Lake." I gazed at him adoringly. Not a moment passed that I didn't feel incredibly fortunate to live another day with Daniel by my side. The chance to experience this kind of unconditional and all-consuming love was truly a gift from the gods, the universe, or whatever the source for such powerful emotions. I would never take it for granted. Never.

"This time, I think we can both agree that Althea saved you," Daniel said.

I gripped his hand. "Her snakes are alive, right? The hemlock didn't kill any of them, did it?"

Daniel touched my cheek gently. "It was only a small amount of hemlock. Plus, she made sure to use enough snakes that no single snake ingested too much of the poison. She's one smart Gorgon."

"And I was one lucky sorceress," I added. "If we hadn't been in my office, Althea wouldn't have been able to save me." I would've never forgiven myself if anything had happened to one of her snakes. Even though I was firmly in the Indiana Jones camp when it came to snakes, I had no desire to sacrifice any of her girls to save me.

Daniel stroked the skin on the back of my hand and my whole body tingled. "You can't die on me, Emma. I have big plans to grow old with you."

From his perch, Sedgwick groaned. *I'd rather roll my feathers in tar than listen to this drivel.*

"You're an angel," I replied, ignoring my familiar. "Growing old will take a very long time."

"I sure hope so." The intensity of his gaze warmed me from head to toe. "So what happened to Tomlin?"

"Astrid managed to take him into custody before the freeze spell wore off," Gareth interjected. I'd been too busy swooning over my fiancé to realize he was back in the room.

My good mood quickly soured. "Poor Tomlin."

Daniel reeled back. "You can't be serious. He killed Seamus and then he tried to kill you to cover it up."

"Aye, he doesn't deserve your pity," Gareth agreed.

"Killing Seamus was an accident," I said. "He was trying to make amends with his friend. He was trying to be better."

"There is no try," Daniel said. "Only do."

I patted his cheek. "My pop-culture references are rubbing off on you."

He kissed my forehead. "One of these days, I'm actually going to see one of the films you reference."

I thought about the secret lair with its magic mirror. I couldn't take him there. The remedial witches would cry foul.

I smiled vaguely. "We'll figure something out." I decided to broach my reception idea with him while he was in a good mood.

"The whole town?" he repeated, incredulous.

"We can afford it," I argued. "And it would be so much fun to include everyone."

"This isn't a primary school birthday party," Gareth interjected. "You don't need to include everyone."

"I know, but I want to," I told him. "I've met so many paranormals since I've moved here and every single one has left a lasting impression."

"You're even going to invite Sheriff Hugo?" Daniel asked. "His lasting impression isn't so positive."

Former Sheriff Hugo," I said. "And, yes, even him. If he doesn't want to come, that's his decision."

"And what about *former* Mayor Knightsbridge?' Daniel queried. "I have no doubt she'd cause trouble for us."

"She's under house arrest, remember?" I said. "She wouldn't be allowed to come under the terms of her arrangement." Unless her petition for early release was granted, of course, but I didn't want to worry Daniel with that tidbit.

Daniel threaded his fingers through mine. "Sounds like you've got it all figured out, Miss Smartypants."

Overachiever, Sedgwick griped from his perch in the corner of the room.

I kissed my angel lightly on the lips. "Not all, but it's fun to try."

Now that the wedding plans were coming together and Tomlin's case was closed, I finally gathered the courage to read through the rest of my mother's letters. I sat on the sofa with my legs tucked underneath my bottom, absorbing every finely curved word.

Gareth floated into the room with a cup of tea and set it on the end table. "For you."

I beamed at him. "Thanks. I still can't believe how well you're doing with the physical world."

He gave a mock bow. "You're not the only overachiever in the house, you know."

Magpie came tearing into the room and leaped onto the arm of the sofa, his tail nearly knocking over the cup. I grabbed it before it toppled over.

"That's not for you," I said firmly.

"He saw me carrying it," Gareth said sheepishly. "I suppose he expected the contents of the cup to be for him."

"Talk about spoiled." I stuck out my tongue at Magpie and he hissed in response, before jumping to the floor.

"How far have you gotten with the letters?" Gareth hovered behind me for a better look at the letter in my hand.

"Not as far as I'd like. I want to know more about her role as Warden of the West. It's all so fascinating. I never expected my mother to be a badass. It's like discovering I'm the secret daughter of Wonder Woman."

Gareth tried to grab the letter, but his hand went straight through the paper. "That's what I get for not focusing my will."

I smiled. "You don't need to hold it. I'll read it out loud for both of us." I cleared my throat.

"Be sure to enunciate," Gareth said. "Sometimes you mumble."

"I do *not* mumble!" I unfolded the next letter and began to read in a loud, clear voice. "My dearest Geri and Barron, I hope this letter finds you and my darling daughter well. I had hoped to send better news of my situation, but, alas, there is no rest for a busy Warden of the West. I was recently handed a difficult case by the Enforcer of the East in Europe. One of his marks managed to escape across the Atlantic and I tracked him as far as what was once Ridge Valley."

"Fancy that," Gareth said. "She mentions the old name for Spellbound."

"It reminds me of another case from long ago, when I was still in training to be a warden. As I am sure you recall, that town remains inaccessible to our kind because of the curse that resulted..."

I stopped reading aloud as my eyes tracked the remainder of the paragraph.

ANNABEL CHASE

"What about the curse?" Gareth prompted. "Did your mother know something that might help us?"

I continued to stare at the remaining words on the page. A lump formed in my throat and I could scarcely draw breath.

"Emma, what does the rest of the letter say?" he implored.

I blinked back tears as I looked my vampire ghost roommate in the eye. "Spell's bells, Gareth. I think my mother is the one who put the curse on Spellbound."

* * *

THANK YOU FOR READING

I hope you enjoyed **Hemlocked and Loaded**! If so, please consider leaving a review on Amazon because they are so important to authors.

You can also sign up for my new releases via e-mail by visiting http://eepurl.com/ctYNzf or like me on Facebook so you can find out about the next book before it's even available.

Don't miss *All Spell Breaks Loose*, Book 10.

You can also check out my new **Starry Hollow Witches** series:

Magic & Murder, Book 1

Magic & Mystery, Book 2

Magic & Mischief, Book 3

Magic & Mayhem, Book 4

Magic & Mercy, Book 5

Made in the USA
Columbia, SC
26 December 2018